THE GYMFATUATION

THE CURVY GIRLS CLUB #2

NIKKI ASHTON

The Gymfatuation
The Curvy Girls Club #2
Copyright © Nikki Ashton 2023

Published by Hudson Indie Ink
www.hudsonindieink.com

The Gymfatuation/Nikki Ashton
ISBN 13 - 978-1-916562-39-4

GYMFATUATION - URBAN DICTIONARY DEFINITION

That **smoking hot** guy or girl you **sneak** stares at while at **the gym**.

*Dude, you're totally gymfatuated with that chick! Stop **staring** and **lift**.*

*Wow, stop staring! Is he your **gymfatuation** or what?*
by Obsidio February 12, 2013

CHAPTER ONE

You know when you decide to do something and immediately regret it? Yep, that was me on my way to the gym. One night when we'd been drunk, off our heads on gin, my friend, Olive, and I had signed up.

If that hadn't been stupid enough, we'd also said we wanted a personal trainer. I mean, why would a woman who always had to go to the back of the shop to buy her clothes and got her bras from places with names like Big n Bouncy, want to go to the bloody gym?

I totally blamed Olive. She was the one who forced the gin down my throat, and it was her laptop that we'd used. As cabin crew she was the one under pressure to stay slim. I worked behind a desk taking calls for an insurance company. The only people who judged me about my size was the little prick who sat next to me at work, Dylan, or Dildo as I liked to call him.

As I parked my little Fiat 500 I looked up at the signage on the front of the gym and sighed.

" *Today is the day you meet your new self.*' What a load of old bollocks," I muttered as I turned off the engine. "My new self my big fat arse." I wasn't searching for my new anything if Olive didn't turn up, and she was late.

Five minutes later, just as I had my finger on the key to start my car, her bright yellow Beetle zoomed into the space next to me. Sighing with relief, I grabbed my towel and bottle of water and got out of the car.

"Sorry, sorry," Olive called over the roof of her car. "Work called about a long haul flight that needs a crew."

"When?" I demanded, my heart dropping to my stomach. "Don't you dare tell me it's any time this week. We've signed up for three training sessions and I'm not doing it if you're not going to be here."

"I'll be here." She pulled her long blonde hair into a messy bun but averted her gaze.

"Olive," I snapped out her name. "What aren't you telling me?"

She looked at me with a pained expression. "I couldn't say no. It's great money and Daniel is the pilot."

I gasped. "You're abandoning your best friend just so you can have a shag on the other side of the world?" I slapped a hand to my chest like my heart was broken. "I can't believe it."

I mean, I could believe it. Daniel was a super-hot pilot who'd she'd been having sex with for the last six months. They weren't in a relationship as such but were shagging each other exclusively. I'd met him a couple of times and he was genuinely nice. He liked Olive a lot and treated her like a queen, he just didn't want anything serious. Which suited her, seeing as they were rarely in the same place at the same time, unless it was the same flight.

"I'm so sorry, Luisa." She sucked on her bottom lip and

fluttered her eyelashes at me. "I'll bring you some perfume back. That one you really like."

Exhaling, I nodded. "The expensive one?"

"Absolutely."

"And Ouzo?"

"It goes without saying." It was the drink we always bought each other as a thank you or an apology. It was our thing and had been since I'd used it to say sorry for ruining her favourite jumper not long after we became friends.

"Fine," I replied. "But that means you'll be godmother to only *one* of my kids now."

"I totally understand." She nodded and looked suitably chastised.

I glanced over at the gym door. "Shall we sack it off? Go back to mine and watch Naked Attraction instead?"

"No." She frowned. "We're doing this. We agreed."

"Well, yes we did, Olive, but I'm not the one jetting off to…where are you jetting off to by the way?"

"Miami."

I shuddered. "Oh, be careful. Remember last time you went there you ended up with the shits."

"Luisa," she cried. "Really. Do you have to?"

I shrugged. "But you did."

"I know, which is why I'll be avoiding the oysters. Now," she said, impatiently. "Are we going in or not?"

Ooh, she gave me a choice.

I turned to my car door. "Not is perfectly fine with m—"

"Get inside." A hand on my arm tugged me back. "We are going to do this. For once, we're going to do what we said we'd do."

She was right. We were always knocking things on the head before we'd even started them.

"Okay." I sighed and with heavy feet followed her. "Let's

go and find the new us, even if they're as crappy as the old ones."

When Olive heaved open the large glass door, I could have cried because I knew the next two hours were going to be hell.

CHAPTER TWO

T hings had not started off well for me. In fact, you could say it was as bad as shit in a snow globe.

When we reached reception, our Personal Trainer, James, was waiting for us. I didn't know his name was James until he introduced himself and I immediately burst out laughing. Olive nudged me and hissed at me to shut up, but I couldn't stop giggling.

"Is something wrong?" James asked.

"Just that your name is Jim, and you work in a gym." I looked at Olive who had her head in her hands. "Ah come on, it's funny."

James evidently didn't think so, or had heard it many times before, because he handed us both a clipboard and commanded we fill the forms in.

Once we'd done that he showed us around, which wasn't too eventful apart from me tripping over a mat. I almost face planted the crotch of a huge guy lifting weights, but James managed to grab me. When I looked at him to thank him, I could definitely see some trepidation in his eyes, and I wasn't sure ours was going to be a particularly good working relationship.

Tour over, he instructed us in a couple of fitness-check exercises. That was where things went from shit to shittier. The run on the treadmill was bad enough, but then he had us doing burpees. I'm not proud to say when he first mentioned them, I actually let out a belch and grinned proudly. It was a talent of mine being able to burp on demand. And yes, I had tried to get on Britain's Got Talent with it—another drunken idea Olive and I had—but it clearly wasn't what the vetting-people considered a talent.

"Jesus," Olive groaned. "You're such an embarrassment."

"What have I done now?"

"You don't know what a burpee is?" James asked. When I shook my head he gave me the kind of smile you gave your friend's naughty kid. The one you really couldn't stand but had to pretend you liked, because you liked your friend. "I'll show you," he said, and proceeded to pull off some strange movement that only belonged in a circus or a porn film.

I burst out laughing. "I can't do that."

"Just try for me," he said. "Just five."

"Five?" I protested. "Do you want me to die?"

He chuckled softly and I was sure in his head he was saying, 'Yes I do. I really do.'. "You won't die, these are what are known as gentle burpees." There was nothing gentle about them. "Olive, can you do them, do you think?"

Teacher's pet nodded and straightened the straps of her sports bra top.

"Okay, on three."

He counted down and I dropped into a squat. By the time I'd heaved myself up to standing again, Olive was already back on the way down. I dropped again, kicked my legs out behind be, brought them back in and stood up. As I started the third one, something didn't feel quite right. There was a bit of a cold draught around the midriff area.

"Keep going," James said, clapping his hands enthusiastically. "Well done, Olive. That's great, take a breather."

As I straightened up, I glanced at Olive who I was glad to see was breathing heavily. When I groaned she looked at me and her eyebrows arched.

"Trousers," she snapped.

Instantly I knew what she meant. When I looked, I realised they'd rolled down, my top had rolled up, and my belly was on full display. Sagging in all its glory. I grabbed at the waistband of the Lycra leggings and struggled to unfurl them. Due to the elasticity, though, the harder I tried the more they curled.

"Oh shit."

"Come on," James cried, bending to get on eye level with me. "Just two more, Luisa."

"My stomach is hanging out."

"Don't worry about that. One more."

Giving up trying to regain my dignity, I dropped one more time and completed what was probably the slowest burpee of all time. When I finished I didn't know what to do first. Did I try and get my breath, or did I pull my leggings up to cover my belly and my arse, because that was now also on show?

Deciding I wanted to live a long and happy life, I bent at the knees, breathed in and out and just hoped no one decided to hang their towel from my arse crack.

James had given us a five-minute water break, and I was sure it was more for his benefit than ours. After her initial display of athleticism, Olive went downhill fast. Having a little more weight behind me, I was able to beat her pushing a large piece of equipment across the gym. Don't ask me what the equipment was called, it was just big, heavy, red, and looked a bit like an upside down table with weights threaded on the legs. Buoyed by my success, I was instantly demoralised when we then both sucked at slamming heavy ropes up and down.

"I think I hate him," Olive hissed from the corner of her mouth.

"You've changed your tune." I swallowed back *all* my water before pushing the bottle under the fountain and refilling it. "He is good looking, though."

She shrugged. "His left ear is slightly bigger than his right one."

"How the hell did you notice that?" Another long drink of beautiful cold water went down my throat.

"Being cabin crew, I notice these things."

I thought about it for a moment but chose to ignore it, as I did with the majority of what she said. She was my best friend and I loved her, but she often talked total and utter tripe.

"He's got a very nice bum," I offered. "That makes up for the ear size."

"Not as nice as Daniel's but nice. He's also got very nice forearms. They actually remind me of Daniel's. They have the same eye colour too."

"Yes he does. Well spotted, although having not been intimate with Daniel, I can't comment on the likeness. Nice teeth too. Do they match up to Daniel's?"

She grinned around the lip of her bottle. "No, but I think we'd still get a really good price for him at auction."

"I'd want to keep stud rights, though," I quipped.

"Obviously."

"Right, ladies." James appeared at our sides. "Ready to get going again?'

With a heavy sigh, I pushed away from the wall and started to follow him. Realising that Olive wasn't with us, I turned to see her talking on her phone. Where the hell she'd had that secreted I had no clue, her outfit was skin-tight. I had to put mine in a locker when it fell out of my bra during my run on the treadmill.

"James," I called. "Olive isn't ready."

He turned and frowned. "She'll have to catch us up. I have another client in half an hour."

I was torn with sagging with relief that I only had another half hour of torture to endure, and groaning because there was still another thirty minutes of hell.

"What are we doing now?" I asked as I trailed after him.

He stopped and pointed at a bright yellow cube. "You're going to be climbing on and off that."

I gulped and wondered whether I would be fast enough to escape him if I ran. Gripping my water bottle, I whimpered. "I...I...I can't do that. I've only got little legs."

James looked down my body and grinned. "You've got perfectly normal length legs, it's your body that's short."

My mouth gaped open. "Sorry?"

He started to laugh. "There's nothing wrong with the length of your body either."

"Clearly it's just the width then."

James shook his head and rolled his eyes. "Come on, you can do this."

"I really don't think I can."

He put a hand to my elbow and guided me towards my imminent death.

"Shouldn't we wait for Olive?"

James glanced over his shoulder and frowned. "Well, she's not there, so…" He shrugged. "I think you're on your own."

"What?" I spun around and the place where Olive had stopped to take her call was deserted. She was nowhere to be seen. "Where is she?" Craning my neck, my eyes searched the rest of the gym, and the little witch was gone. "I'll bloody kill her."

"Must have been an emergency," James said. "So, come on."

Following him, I made a mental note to obliterate Olive from my life in every sense. The box was knee high, not quite as big as it looked from a distance, it may well have still been as high as a mountain, though.

"We're going to do two sets of ten on each leg. That's stepping up onto the box and lifting the other leg to your knee once you're up there." Evidently I looked like I had no clue what he was talking about. "Look, let me show you."

He showed me, he made it look easy and I looked again for an escape route.

"When I'm sure that you've got your balance, we'll introduce some weights." He planted his feet a hip's width apart and folded his arms over his chest. "Off you go."

Giving him a withering look, I placed one foot on the box and heaved myself up, pushing my hands in the air and bringing my other knee up. Wobbling, I quickly stepped down and repeated the action. It seemed that my right leg had a lot more wobble in it than my left one. As soon as I lifted my arms, I lost my balance and with a whoop fell backwards.

"Shit."

"Woah!" James cried.

My foot went off the end of the box and I waited for the inevitable thump as I hit the ground. Only I didn't. Instead, I fell against a hard, extremely hard, *exceptionally hard*, body. Tanned, veined, forearms wrapped around my stomach, steadying me as he took a half step back.

"You okay?" he asked, his breath tickling my ear, his arms tightening around me. "Did you hurt yourself?"

Did I hurt myself? Why would I hurt myself? Oh yes, because I'd fallen off a stupid bloody box.

It had skipped my mind because I was so distracted by the hard body and tanned forearms. It was obvious I had damsel in distress syndrome, or something like that, because now there were butterflies swooping in my belly. Said belly which was being held by the tanned forearms.

"I'm…er…I'm fine, thanks." When James loosened his grip on me, I wished I'd said I was hurt or that my nipples had been injured and maybe he should check them out.

Taking me by the shoulders, he turned me around and stooped to look in my eyes. "You sure nothing hurts. Nothing that I need to take a look at?"

"My vag—" Sense kicked in and I shook my head. "My vague recollection is that I just lost balance."

I personally thought it was a great save, but James was looking at me like I was about to throw him to the ground and ravish him. I mean, I would have but we'd only just met and… well, it didn't seem right in the middle of a busy gym.

"Honestly, I'm fine."

His broad shoulders sagged with relief. "I think we'll call it a day for today. Go and grab a drink, take a seat for a few minutes before you think about driving, and I'll see you in a couple of days for your next session."

Frowning, I stooped down to pick up my water bottle. "Next session?"

"Yeah, you signed up for six for starters. Three this week and three next." He reached for his clipboard and flicked through some papers. "Oh, and the bootcamp that I hold at Denmere Forest."

I gulped and almost dropped my bottle of water.

"B-boot camp?"

"Two days of core strength exercising and some cardio." He grinned like his two days of hell was the best invention of the millennium. I had to disagree but as usual was too bloody chicken to do it.

I just wished our conversation had been through text messages. I'd have had the perfect response to his bloody boot camp. Memes were invaluable when you didn't have that perfect comeback.

"I'm not sure that I can make it now," I replied. "I have a wedding that weekend."

James narrowed his eyes on me. "What *date* would that be?" His top lip twitched, and he was undoubtedly onto me.

Shit. I had no clue what I'd signed up for. I'd been drinking gin and lots of it.

"The date would be… er… that would be." I grimaced. "The sixth?"

"Well, you're in luck. The boot camp is next weekend on the evening of fourteenth until the afternoon of the sixteenth. And your wedding is on a Thursday, interesting."

He was definitely onto me.

"Yes," I replied, nodding my head slowly. "They're a very Avant Garde couple, Justin and Hailey."

James nodded slowly. "Hailey and Justin? Right."

"Yep. That's right. Hailey and Justin er Beaver."

Oh. My. God. Why didn't I just learn to keep my mouth shut? Why did I always keep talking until I sounded like some sort of half-wit?

"Well, I hope the Beavers have a lovely wedding day. *And*

it's great that you'll still be able to come to boot camp. Work off some of that wedding cake."

Sighing heavily, I nodded, resigned to spending my last days running around some woods while pumping weights. I supposed there was one consolation, a certain pair of chocolate brown eyes might be the last I looked into.

CHAPTER THREE

L ying back in the bath, I ignored my phone when it rang for the fifth time. It was Olive and I was still pissed off at her. She'd just disappeared on me, and I didn't even want to go to the bloody gym. It had been her idea. I'd let her use the keyboard, so she'd been the one who signed us up for the bloody boot camp. A boot camp that she wouldn't even be going to because she'd be flat on her back in Miami with her muffin gettin' a stuffin' by Daniel.

No, I was ignoring her and letting her think about her actions. Because she'd not only let me down, but she'd also let herself down, and she'd let her parents down.

Too much? Yeah, well she deserved it.

Taking a sip of wine, I thought back to the hour and a half of torment I'd gone through earlier. It was hideous and the only saving grace was James, or Gym Jim, as I'd decided to store him as in my phone. When I'd gone to get myself a drink and calm myself after my accident—okay, stumble—he went with me. Checking I was okay, he sat with me for five minutes and we chatted about life. To be honest, what he actually said was that he working until nine that night and would miss the football on the telly.

When he'd been torturing me, I'd not appreciated his beauty, but watching him then had given me an opportunity to study him in more depth. My conclusion was, he was extremely good looking and I could easily form a little crush on him. With deep brown eyes, the colour of rich, strong coffee beans, and a little dimple in his strong jaw, James wouldn't have looked out of place in an advert for an energy drink. I could see him shirtless, in gym shorts that rested on his hips, while he swigged back a blue drink that gave him the energy to shag you for hours.

It had been a while since I'd had a man's hands on me. In fact, my teal and gold coloured vibrator with five speeds '*including the awesome clit tickler*', had been the only source of my orgasms for the last eight months. Actually...

Thinking about having an orgasm along with James' bulging biceps, had given me another idea to help me relax.

I sat up and leaned over to open the wooden cabinet in which I stored toilet rolls. Pushed at the back, in what looked like a washbag, was my waterproof bathroom dildo. It might seem strange, but as a single woman I liked to be prepared for every eventuality. I didn't want to be lying in bed and wondering where I'd left my vibrator. Or when I was in the bath and fancied a quick play with my clam-hat, I did not want to have to slop water all down the landing to my bedroom to get my vibrator, only to have lost the urge once I got back into my then tepid bathwater.

"Hello, my little friend," I said as I pulled the vibrator from the bag.

Turning it on, the familiar thrill rushed through me, and I briefly considered the sadness of it. I wasn't even thirty and yet the most sexual excitement I had was from a bloody a rechargeable piece of rubber. It didn't escape me that I was in my prime and should be being worshipped by a real man on a regular basis. That, instead of parting my thighs and touching myself while imagining a topless Charlie Hunnam hovering over me, I should have been listening to a man tell me how beautiful I was. Not hearing a constant buzzing noise.

Hooking one leg on the side of the bath, I put my head back, closed my eyes and lowered the vibrator into the water. The first touch was good, as usual, sending an initial wave of pleasure through my body making my nipples stand to attention. Circling the vibrator around my bundle of nerves, I groaned softly. I was not a woman who needed a lot of attention to orgasm. Coming hard and loud was normal for me, even if it was of my own making. Multiple orgasms were not unknown, which was why it was disappointing that I didn't have a man to benefit from my ability to explode like an over-filled firework.

Needing more pressure, I pushed the vibrator hard against my clit and squeezed my thighs together. The waves built from the depth of my stomach and washed through me, each pulse getting stronger as they merged. I pushed the vibrator inside of me and pressed on the dimpled button to change the speed and the pattern. With my orgasm gaining momentum, I thrust the vibrator in and out. The warm water lapped against my skin like a gentle touch as I started to pant hard, my breath the only sound echoing around the bathroom.

"Oh, god," I gasped as my whole body tingled with the pleasure. When I moved the vibrator back to my clit, I instantly fell over the edge and screamed out my release. Thrusting my hips, water splashed over the side of the bath onto the floor, and I breathed through the ripples, coming hard.

"Wow," I gasped, dropping the vibrator onto the floor.

"That was fun." Sated and relaxed, I closed my eyes. "Thanks, Charlie."

The best thing, Charlie didn't answer back, and he didn't complain about me staying in the bath for another half an hour either.

———

Wearing my PJ's, feet up and eating ice cream—rum and raisin, obviously—I groaned when my doorbell rang.

"Go away," I muttered under my breath.

Whoever it was evidently wasn't listening and kept their finger on the bell. The insistent shrill was annoying to say the least, so I had no choice but to slam my ice cream down and stomp down the hall.

Through the glass in the doorway, I could make out Olive's outline lit up against the light from her mobile phone. My mobile rang from the living room, so it didn't take much to guess it was me she was calling.

Sighing, I flung the door open. "Will you stop pressing the bloody bell?"

"Oh, you answered." She gave a little shrug and held out a bottle of wine. "Sorry."

She was annoying as hell, but I could never stay mad with her for long, especially when she came baring gifts of alcohol.

"You'd better come in."

Slipping past me, she paused to kick off her Crocs. "I am sorry."

"You said." I closed the door, grabbed the wine from her and walked back to the lounge. "Grab some glasses from the kitchen and put that hideous footwear in the cupboard under the stairs. I will not have them being seen from the door."

"Who are you expecting at the door to even see them?" she called, making her way down the hallway.

"No one, but I'm not willing to risk my reputation. Oh, and bring a spoon if you want ice cream." Plonking myself back on the sofa, I stretched out my legs and settled back down. I unscrewed the top off the wine and took a quick smell. I was no expert, but Olive had been known to buy vinegar masquerading as wine on many occasions. It didn't smell too acidic thankfully.

"Here." Olive appeared in front of me and handed me a glass. "It's a good one, I paid almost a fiver for it."

That statement said it all. For a woman who travelled all over the world, drinking and eating in some of the best restaurants, she had terrible taste buds.

"Don't you want ice cream?"

She screwed up her face and fake gagged. "Rum and raisin is the flavour of the devil."

I rest my case.

"Where did you go?" I asked, pouring myself a glass of wine. "You just disappeared."

"Daniel called."

I rolled my eyes, having a good idea what she was about to say. "Let me guess, he had a short stopover in Manchester and was on your doorstep desperate for a shag."

Distracted by something on the rim of her glass, Olive grunted confirmation.

"Has he gone now?"

Seemingly satisfied it wasn't anything too nasty, she took a sip of wine before saying, "Yes, he left about an hour ago." She sighed and snuggled up against a cushion. "He said that he can't wait for us to get to Miami. We've got a three day layover, so he's got a load of stuff planned for us."

"Yeah," I muttered. "Lay being the operative word."

"No," she snapped, pulling her legs up. "We're going to have a surf lesson."

My head snapped up. "He booked that for you?" Olive was obsessed with the idea of being able to surf and was always harping on about it, even though we lived in a city.

"Yep." She said that one little word so proudly that I knew she was totally gone for Daniel the pilot. Sadness overwhelmed me because I also knew that one day I'd probably lose her to him. Then she'd be gone, living in some big house in Surrey. I wanted that for Olive, but I also wanted it for myself. Not Surrey though, those people in the south had no idea how to make a decent cup of tea.

"So, do you remember signing us up for a boot camp?"

Blinking slowly, it wasn't long before the memory clearly came flooding back to her. "Shit. I did, didn't I?"

"Yes you did. Which means while you're cutting waves, I'll be running up bloody mountains and carrying logs heavier than my own body weight, and that is something."

Olive scowled, as she always did when I was self-deprecating about my size. "Don't be stupid."

"Seriously, I will be running up mountains."

Reaching out, Olive poked at my leg with her foot and muttered something about me being a dick head. Bright red toenails matched her ankle length jeans and lipstick and I marvelled at just how put together she was—*and* she'd just been shagged for hours. I regularly looked like an unmade bed when I was at home, but Olive was always ready and primed for an unexpected visitor or night out.

She glared at me. "You are going aren't you?" she asked, pulling her leg back. "You better not have told him that something has come up."

I grimaced, recalling the Beaver wedding which I'd be

attending and ruing the fact that she knew me so well. "I tried but he kind of backed me into a corner."

Olive burst out laughing. "Ha, you wish he'd back you into a corner. Back you into it then bonk the life out of you. And good for him, not taking your shit."

I didn't deny I liked the idea of a shag, because despite my orgasm earlier, my sexual appetite hadn't been dulled. I could totally get on board with Gym Jim having his way with me.

"You'll be okay you know," she said, softly encouraging.

"I guess we'll soon find out."

"God, I'm so sorry, Lu. I honestly wouldn't have abandoned you if—"

"If the man you're falling in love with hadn't offered you three days in heaven." I couldn't blame her really.

"As long as you don't hate me." She pouted prettily and I rolled my eyes, before offering a smile. It didn't escape my notice that she hadn't denied the fact she was falling in love.

"I don't hate you."

"And you promise me you'll go? No backing out like you usually do?"

I rolled my eyes. "No backing out, I promise." God, I hated when she made me promise. She knew I could never and would never break one.

"Good. Besides, I paid for it on your credit card, and you don't want to waste the money. Now," she flashed me a grin, "tell me, how good is this wine?"

It wasn't. It was awful but I didn't want to piss on her parade. She had a good heart really and for her to spend almost a fiver on wine only went to prove how much she loved me.

"It's good," I lied. "Now, tell me how many times you got jiggy jiggy this afternoon and in what positions."

While Olive regaled her sexual tales, I tried to quell the nervousness which had reared up in my stomach. I was going to be doing something way beyond my comfort zone. Not only that, but I was also going to be doing it with people I didn't know and the idea of not having Olive, my cheerleader, with me, scared the shit out of me. But, like the dick head I was, I'd made a promise and I had to stick by it.

CHAPTER FOUR

"Well done," James said as I collapsed in a heap. He patted my head and chuckled. "Come on, on your feet."

"You're cruel," I groaned. "Let me just stay here."

He crouched down beside me and placed a hand between my sweaty shoulder blades. "You only managed three chin ups last time. Five is a great improvement and deserves a treat."

My head shot up and I saw that he was grinning at me. "What like? A foot massage or a large glass of gin and tonic?"

"No, but you can have a water and an energy bar." He stood up and held out his hand. "It's on me."

I rolled my eyes because water and energy bars were free, but I still took the offer of his help to get up off the floor. Once I was up, he gave me a little nudge towards the small café at the back of the gym.

"Take a seat and I'll get us something to drink."

Glad of the rest, I headed for a table which was right next to the window. Mainly because it had comfy armchairs but also because it had a good view of the local park. I was surprised how busy it was for a mid-week. There were kids playing football, people walking dogs, and a few joggers on the path around the outside. There were some swings and a slide in one corner, and I could see a bunch of teenage girls had commandeered the swings while some boys hung around the slide. Clearly it was the epicentre of the teenage dating scene, so not much had changed over the years.

"Here you go."

When James placed a mug of coffee down on the table I was surprised. "I thought I was getting water, or at least a freshly squeezed orange juice."

He grinned and shoved his hand into his short's pocket before producing an energy bar. "I think you deserve it. You've worked hard tonight."

I looked at the clock on the wall to see that it wasn't quite seven and so I still had half an hour left of my session. "I might make this coffee last me half an hour," I joked.

"That's fine." James unscrewed the cap on a bottle of water and took a swig. I was fixated watching him and when some dripped onto his chest I made a funny little moany noise. The kind I might have made if he'd taken me up on that foot massage I'd wanted.

Quickly, I took a sip of my coffee, hoping my moan hadn't been as loud as it had been in my head. When James put the bottle on the table and wiped the back of his mouth with his hand, I was relieved when he didn't get up and leave or ask me to stop making pervy sex noises while watching him drink.

"I think we can spend the rest of the session here," he said, surprising me.

"Really?"

"Yep. You've done well today and besides I don't want you getting an injury before the weekend."

He smiled and I grimaced.

The dreaded boot camp.

"Don't look so scared," he said, pushing the energy bar across the table. "I won't make you do anything you don't want to do."

"So, I don't need to go at all, then?"

He cocked his head on one side and gave me a wry smile. "You're not getting out of it that easily."

"Believe me, there's going to be nothing easy about me doing boot camp."

"Honestly, you'll be fine."

He patted my hand which was laid flat on the table, and I was surprised by the little shiver it caused, like he'd blown a soft whisper over my skin. I mentally shook it off. He was a hottie and fit, and I had no chance with my extra rolls of fat on my stomach and padding on my bum. I knew I was pretty but pretty and plump wasn't a combination many men went for.

I'd dated a big guy once. Scott had a big tummy, legs, and thighs and he loved food and beer. He wasn't the archetypal handsome guy, but he made me laugh and for a month made me happy, and the sex was pretty good. Then he one night he said to me that I wasn't his usual type and me being naïve asked if he usually went for blondes, as I was brunette. When he said, 'No, big girls. I usually like them slim but when I met you, I thought why not give it a try.', I knew that would be our last date. Scott and a few men before him who *hadn't* 'given me a try', were who told me that I didn't have a chance with James.

"What made you become a personal trainer?" I asked,

shaking off thoughts of Scott and pushing the energy bar to one side.

James sat back in his chair and sighed. "I was a really, really fat kid. And I mean really fat."

"No way." I stared at him with wide eyes, trying to see where there may have been some fat.

He nodded. "Up until I was sixteen. I wasn't good academically either so had no clue what I wanted to do with my life. Which meant when me and my mates left school they all had a plan, and I didn't. They were mostly going on to college or sixth form, except for my very best friend Tom, he was going to work for his dad."

"You must have felt lost," I replied. "I know I did because I was the same, but it was when I was eighteen, after college."

"Exactly that. I thought they were all moving on and I was the fat one left behind. It didn't help that my brother was a bloody genius."

"So, what did you do?"

"My dad and mum were great and told me I could enjoy my last summer as a school kid, but once it was over I had to find a job. Which meant a lot of evenings were spent looking for something for when adulthood began." He scratched the back of his neck and grinned. "I have to be honest, most of my time on the internet looking for employment was spent watching porn."

I shrugged. "Haven't we all done that? I used to tell my mum and dad I was watching makeup tutorials."

James' eyebrows shot up as he blinked rapidly, and I wondered if I'd taken a step too close to inappropriate. It was true, though, and I thanked those videos for my perfect smoky eye and amazing blow-job skills.

A thought struck me, and I leaned across the table and

whispered, "Did you lose weight by watching porn?" If he had, then maybe that was my next new diet plan.

"No." He laughed, shaking his head and looking at me with a strangely soft look on his face. "I happened to come across some workout videos so started to do them in the evening. Then I figured there was no point if I wasn't eating properly, so cut out all the shit that I'd always used to counterbalance the fruit and veg Mum used to make me eat. By the end of the summer, I'd lost over twelve kilos." I frowned and James chuckled. "Two stone. I still had at least another two to go, but it gave me the confidence to apply to college to do a health and wellbeing course. I also joined the gym and when I struggled to get another stone off, I got myself a PT, Matt." He shrugged like what he'd achieved had been nothing, but I was totally in awe of him.

I'd never had the willpower or dedication to do anything like that. My mindset had always been, even though I was overweight, I was fairly healthy and happy so what did it matter? It was only what other people thought about me that messed with my head.

"Did you do your PT training after that?" I asked.

James nodded. "Yeah, it's almost nine years now. And one day maybe I'll have my own gym, or at least a Tranter franchise."

"Tranters are a franchise?"

"Yes. Freddie Tranter started off with one gym in a shitty old building and is now a millionaire." He took a swig of his water before leaning forward, his forearms on the table. "What about you? What do you do?"

I scoffed. "I have a crappy job working for an insurance company. In fact, it's a *very* crappy job and I share my work station with a *very crappy* human being."

I physically shivered and James began to laugh. "Why are they so bad?"

"Because *he* is dick head who likes to call me Lumpy Luisa."

James' mouth dropped open and his grip tightened around his bottle of water. It was so tight I heard the plastic crack.

"*He what*?"

"Yeah." I nodded. "But it's fine. While he was on holiday I helped one of his clients. They re-insured, took out a life policy and made a will and instead of getting them to wait a couple of days until Dylan was back, I did it for them. Which," I said, wiggling my eyebrows, "meant that I got the commission, and it was huge."

"Really?" He was smiling, so clearly didn't think I was a heinous bitch.

"Yes, really. It was so *huge* it paid off my credit card, paid for a week in Spain for my mum and dad and for me to put a deposit on my car."

"Good for you."

Wow, James really did have gorgeous eyes. When he smiled, they twinkled like rays of the sun creating diamonds on the ocean. Shit, what was wrong with me? Why was I getting all poetic and soppy for the man who tortured me three times a week?

"Well, that's what you get when you mess with me," I said, trying to look sinister.

It clearly didn't work because James was laughing again. "You know," he said. "I think we might have a lot of fun at boot camp."

I shuddered at the mere mention of it. "I don't."

"You might be surprised."

"I'll only be surprised if I'm still alive at the end of it."

He leaned further across the table, stretching his arms out

so that his fingertips were close to mine. "Don't underestimate yourself, Luisa," he said, his brow furrowed as he studied me. "You've done so well this last couple of weeks, and we don't know the level of fitness of all the other people. You may be further into your fitness regime than them."

"I doubt it. And let's be clear, I'm here because of Olive."

"But you're here and have stuck to your commitment."

"And they'll probably all still be fitter than me," I exclaimed.

James gave me a look that I'd seen on my dad many times before. Once had been when I'd purposefully punctured the tyre on my bike. I didn't think I would pass my cycling proficiency test so had stuck a nail in it. Dad knew what I'd done and why, and turned up at school with my bike just before the test was about to start. I'd almost had a ten-year-old tantrum in the playground but Luke Johnson, my secret crush, was watching from his mountain bike. So, I accepted my bike from my dad with all the grace I could muster, and I passed.

"Okay, okay," I said, holding my hands up in surrender. "I might be the fittest person there and run rings around them."

"Exactly," James replied with a grin. "And even if you're not, I'll be proud of you, no matter what."

And, oh my god, didn't that leave a warm fuzzy feeling inside that had nothing to do with the hot coffee I gulped down.

CHAPTER FIVE

wo more personal training sessions had not prepared me for what I was about to do.

"You'll be fine," Olive said on the other end of the line.

"Do you think so?" I glanced at my rucksack propped against my bedroom wall and a new wave of nausea hit me. "What if I'm totally shit?"

"James told you that there are varying degrees of ability. He also told you that you can take it at your own pace."

He had told me both of those things, but it still didn't stop my nerves. I was about to set off for James' boot camp with six strangers, oh, and James.

"Call me when you can, but I'm going back to bed to catch up on my sleep." As if on cue she yawned. It wasn't yet seven in Miami, but I'd needed a pep talk before I drove to Wales for the camp. Booking-in was in a few hours but I was going to stop for some lunch on the way and just generally take my time. "My sleep and my orgasms," she whispered with a giggle.

"Stop boasting." The chilled-out zone which 'Charlie' my vibrator had put me in, had worn off. The idea that an orgasm might quell my nerves was real, but I didn't have time, nor the inclination to undress. I was not a woman who could relax into an orgasm while fully dressed. "And say hello to Daniel for me."

"I will. Love you and take care."

"Love you too."

"Oh, and Lu."

"Yeah."

"Don't give up. Promise?"

"Oli—"

"No arguing with me, Luisa. We talked about this, and you promised you'd go through with it." She paused and I knew she'd done it so I could argue, so I didn't. I remained silent and she started up again. "If at the end of the weekend you've hated every minute, then we won't go back to the gym. Do you promise me?"

"You're being unfair, Olive. You were the one who got pissed and signed us up for the bloody thing."

"I know, but now you're in it, stick to it. The boot camp at least." She paused again. Again, I stayed quiet. "*Lu*? You did promise, remember?"

"Okay, okay. I remember that I promised. I'll stick with it."

Olive and her bloody promises! Ugh!

"Good girl."

Since when did she become my mother?

We ended the call, and I flopped back on my bed with a groan. Why the hell was I doing something I didn't want to do? Why? Because of my lack of ability to say no. I'd always found it hard, preferring instead to come up with some ridiculous excuse, Justin and Hailey Beaver's wedding for example.

Never mind getting fit, I needed to get more assertive.

And of course, Olive had made me promise to do it and I never broke a promise.

Looking at the ceiling and noticing I'd missed a pretty large cobweb on my cleaning spree the day before, I considered just not going. I didn't have to go to the gym ever again. I could block Gym Jim's number. I could dye my hair and change my name. I could lie to Olive, or maybe ghost her for the rest of our lives.

"Ah fuck it." I pushed up off the bed, stood, and shook out my limbs. "You can do this."

I seriously doubted whether I could, but I was going to give it a good go. What was the worst thing that could happen?

The worst thing that could happen was that I'd be sleeping in a grotty old cabin, on a tiny wooden bed, with three other people in the same room and a shower in the corner with a mouldy old curtain around it. Those were the worst things that could happen and *had* happened.

"You'll get used to it," James said with a chuckle. "But at least you get first pick on the bed." He scratched his head and grimaced.

The consolation was small, but it was something in the darkness of the musty, dark cabin.

"I'll take the one over there." I pointed to one in the corner. I figured if an axe murderer came in during the night, I'd be the last one he'd reach. It would buy me time to get away and raise the alarm.

"Good choice." James winked at me, and something fluttered in my stomach. "You don't get the draught from the door."

Heaving my backpack on my shoulder, I shuffled past James and the other beds to my preferred choice in the corner. There was a duvet rather than a sleeping bag, which I was pleased about. Not being small meant I tended to look and feel like an overpacked sausage sleeping in one, plus, I couldn't turn over because the whole thing came with me.

"Sorry the bedding looks like it's from the eighties," James said, reaching down to rub his hand over the faded cover with red, blue, and yellow chevrons. "It's clean, though, I promise."

I smiled because I wasn't sure what else to say. I was out of my comfort zone and thought that anything I might say could come across as rude. I mean, how did you say, 'are you sure you didn't steal it from a homeless person?' and not make it sound impolite?

"Okay, Luisa." James pointed over his shoulder with his thumb. "I'll leave you to it. Dinner is at seven in the large building to the left, just past the male cabin. I'm guessing your cabin mates will be here soon. Let me remind myself who you're sharing with." He took out his phone and scrolled through. "There is Saffron, Romy and," he paused and frowned, "Minky."

I spluttered out a laugh. "Shit, sorry." Slapping my hand over my mouth, I had to wonder how the hell I was going to call her Minky and keep a straight face.

"Hey," he replied with a shake of his head. "Don't be sorry, I had to do a double take myself and I've been looking at the name for three weeks."

"No, it's not nice. I promise I won't laugh in front of her."

His soft smile had those wings fluttering in my stomach again. "If you swear not to laugh, well, neither will I."

I gave him a salute. "Guide's honour."

This time his smile was crooked but was just as hot as his

soft one. It made his eyes twinkle and I wondered whether he was a lot of fun when he wasn't yelling at me to put in an extra fifty-percent effort on the treadmill. When I flicked out my tongue and ran it along my lower lip, the twinkle disappeared and was replaced with an intensity which took my breath away. The rich brown of his irises suddenly seemed more black in colour, and just looking at them made my heartbeat speed up.

The silence hung between us for a second and I wasn't sure what to do or say. I didn't dare move in case it spoiled the moment. When there was a knock, the spell was broken. James turned to face the door, and I lost sight of the beautiful eyes which seemed to offer so much.

"Hello," James called.

The door opened and a blonde girl strolled in, pulling a huge pink suitcase behind her. "Oh, please tell me this isn't where we're sleeping for the weekend."

"This isn't where we're sleeping for the weekend," I offered.

James laughed and shook his head. "I'm afraid it is. And while I can't promise you there won't be any spiders, it is pretty clean."

The girl cocked a perfect eyebrow, pursing her lips and looking like she had stomach ache. Although, my guess was we'd *all* have stomach ache by the end of the weekend. I wasn't sure anyone would want to use the toilets if they were as rustic as the sleeping accommodation. Holding it in might be the best option. I didn't even think I'd be taking a shower seeing as I had a phobia about catching a verruca.

"I'm not sure this is what my trainer signed me up for," the girl said. "I'm going to have to call him." She pulled her phone from her large, expensive looking handbag and tapped at the screen with her extra-long nails.

"Who is your trainer?" James asked.

"Adam at Bennetts."

"Ah, you're Minky." James rubbed a hand over his mouth. I knew it was to hide his smile and that made me grin.

"I am and this," she said circling her finger, "is not what I was expecting."

"It's really charming," I offered. "And it has its own ensuite." I pointed to the shower.

"Oh my god! No!" She threw her hands in the air. "I can't possibly shower in that. I need to speak to Adam." She rushed out, slamming the door behind her.

James blinked and shrugged his shoulders. "Well, there's one thing," he said, crossing his arms over his very broad chest. "Minky will be known as Manky by the end of the weekend."

It was then I knew that Gym Jim was my kind of man.

CHAPTER SIX

B y the time dinner came around, I was feeling a little less uncomfortable. Saffron and Romy were lovely, and both had mentioned how nervous they were. I wasn't sure why Romy was, she was clearly fit as she swam for a local club competitively.

"I can't run for shit, though," she said, while pulling her hair into a high ponytail. "My coach says I need to improve my stamina, hence why I'm here."

"I'm sure you'll do better than me," I groaned, poking at my podgy stomach. "I've got this thing and my huge arse to drag around."

"You're very pretty, though."

After having a mini meltdown, Minky had eventually come back with a feather pillow and a twenty-tog duvet she'd had her parents bring to her.

"Sorry?" I asked, knowing exactly what she was getting at.

"You've a very pretty face, you know, for a bigger girl," she replied unashamedly.

"Mindy," Romy gasped. "Don't be so rude."

"It's Minky," Minky replied with a heavy sigh of boredom, clearly used to people getting her name wrong.

"It's fine, Romy." I shrugged. "I'm used to comments like that."

"It's not fine."

"What?" Minky asked. "I was giving her a compliment."

"I call it a shit sandwich," Saffron muttered, as she continued to place items into one of the small chest of drawers we each had next to our beds.

"She is pretty, though." Minky flicked her long blonde hair over her shoulder, her back rigid and defiant. "Romy," she gasped. "Are you saying she isn't? Because if you are, *that's* rude."

"No, I agree, Luisa is very pretty. She pretty and sexy and actually seems like a lovely person. Her being pretty isn't the consolation prize that you seem to think it is."

"I'm not sure I'm sexy," I responded, grimacing with the idea of it.

"Oh yes you are. Very sexy," Romy added. "The way James was watching you on the tour of the camp makes me believe he thinks so, too."

Woah, well that was a surprise. "He wasn't watching me."

Saffron held her hand up. "I second Romy. I saw him looking at your arse."

"He wasn't!" Minky and I both chorused at the same time.

"He was," Romy replied, turning her back on the blonde Princess lounging on her flipping deluxe goose down duvet. "Even if he wasn't, there's no need for her to be so disrespectful. And you," she said, pointing at me, "shouldn't accept those sorts of comments."

I groaned inwardly. I loved that she was rooting for me, but sometimes sticking up for the fat girl was equally as condescending. I could fight my own battles. At least I could when I could be bothered.

"All I'm saying," Minky continued, "is that just because she's overweight, she shouldn't undervalue herself."

"I don't." I looked around Romy so I could see Minky in her size ten body. "I just happen to know that I'm overweight and that I could probably fit two of you in my clothes. That doesn't mean I undervalue myself." That was a lie. I did, on occasion, undervalue myself. If I saw two men laughing I would assume it was me they were laughing at. If another woman looked at me for longer than ten seconds, in my mind, it was always because they were noticing how big I was.

At five feet eight in height and between a size eighteen and twenty, I thought I was huge compared to most girls. Think Arnold Schwarzenegger compared to Danny DeVito in Twins—well, that was how I'd always seen myself. In photographs with friends over the years, I'd always looked like the mother of a group of slim, beautiful, and usually drunk toddlers. It had only been the seven years I'd known Olive that I'd started to get more confidence. From the moment we'd met on our first day at college I knew I loved her.

As we sat down in our very first English Literature lesson, she leaned closer to me and whispered, "Fuck war poets, I'm here for the parties. What about you?"

"Oh my God, same. And because my mum and dad said if I didn't I had to go and work for my dad in his sandwich shop."

"Shit, that's grim. All that tuna mayo and coronation chicken would be enough to make me puke."

I giggled quietly as our lecturer was giving a...well, lecture, about using our mobiles in class. "You'd think I'd love that job, wouldn't you?"

I cracked the joke before she did, but Olive frowned. "Are you supposed to inherit some sort of love for your parent's job then?" Her eyes widened. "Shit, my mum is nurse who does all the cervical smears at the doctor's practice where she works. Does that mean I'll end up liking fanny?"

I burst out laughing and when Olive asked me where I got my top from because it made my tits look awesome, I knew I'd found my person.

Romy sighed heavily, gaining my attention. "Listen, Mindy—"

"It's *Minky*," she cried, frustrated.

"Christ," Saffron muttered, "And you have the cheek to be rude to Luisa when you're named after a set of household items. Were you conceived on an ironing board or something?"

I snorted out a laugh and Saffron gave me a sneaky wink. Romy, however, continued with her tirade.

"Okay, listen, *Minky,* we're going to be spending a lot of time together this weekend, so I think you should apologise to Luisa and consider your words carefully in future."

She blinked twice, crossing her arms over her chest as she waited. Minky huffed and was obviously considering her words carefully because it felt like hours passed before she ground out a, "sorry, Luisa."

"Right," Romy said with a sigh. "Let's get ready for dinner and, just so you know, if we end up playing some sort of truth or dare then Olly is mine."

"Good choice," I replied, grinning, because I agreed he was gorgeous. He was one of four men who were joining us for the weekend.

Olly, who originated from Ghana but had moved to the UK when he was seven, Patrick and Saul, brothers from

Manchester, and Will, a twenty-one year old guy from Shropshire.

"Right, that's good," Saffron said. "Because I'm liking me some of Will."

I didn't want to say anything, but I was sure he was too young for her. I didn't know for certain, but she looked older than him.

"And before you say anything," she added, reading my mind. "I'm twenty-eight and he's legal. Oh, and by the way," she announced to the room, "if anyone needs condoms, I have a box in my bag."

It appeared that there was going to be plenty of exercise of all kinds over the weekend and I only wished I'd packed Charlie. But I guess the poor thing did need a holiday.

CHAPTER SEVEN

The cabin where we had meals was a little larger than the sleeping cabin. It had a long, rustic, wood table which probably sat twenty people on the benches either side. As it was closing in on autumn, there weren't many using the camp, so the room looked even larger than it was. Our small group were camped out at one end of the table and, somehow, I'd found myself sandwiched between Saffron and Will. James was opposite to me, and his attention was being dominated by Minky who was next to him. There was some serious flirtatious banter going across me and so watching James was a great distraction from the vocal sex show going on around me.

James was extremely handsome and the way he listened intently to Minky's conversation about her new Mercedes was cute. He nodded and asked questions and, to all intents and purposes, was interested. I could see, though, that it wasn't really his thing. It was in his eyes. Plus, each time Minky took a breath, he glanced over at me and smiled. A smile which was much brighter and more sincere than those he was giving to her.

I couldn't lie, it made me feel all squidgy inside, which kind of matched the outside. When he rested his forearm on the table, all tanned and wearing a large watch, and he traced the edge of a plate mat with his finger tip, it caused a little swoop in my stomach. So enthralled in his left limb I didn't notice that Minky had got up from the table or that James was calling my name.

"Luisa. Hey, Luisa."

Roused from my daydream, my gaze shot to his. "Oh, sorry, did you say something?"

"I was asking if you're okay about tomorrow?"

I barked out a loud laugh, causing Olly and Patrick to pause their conversation. "Sorry," I mouthed before turning back to James. "Am I okay about tomorrow?"

He smiled and my eyes were drawn to his mouth, and how both his incisors were slightly longer that the rest of his teeth. Weirdly, I found it quite sexy. I could imagine them sinking into my neck and him drinking from me and me... woah, who knew that I had a thing for vampires? I'd always been Team Jacob, but my taste had clearly changed.

"I take it that it's a no," he said.

"Not a no as such. More shit scared really."

His brow furrowed. "Why? I'm not going to make you do anything that you're not comfortable with or capable of."

"I'm not capable of much, so I guess it'll be a quiet few days for me."

James shook his head. "Oh, no. You've done well the last couple of PT sessions. Your fitness is already making progress."

"Already?" I questioned. "I doubt that."

"You'd be surprised. Your step ups were quicker by six seconds on your last session."

"Wow, six seconds." I sighed. "Is that a magical six

seconds, you know like a man will tell you this is six inches?" I held my forefinger and thumb the tiniest distance apart and grinned.

His top lip twitched in amusement. "I can assure you, Luisa," he said in a low voice. "When I show you six inches, it'll be a real six inches."

And that was when heat flooded my body, and my knickers got a little bit damper.

After dinner we sat around chatting, until James finally slammed his palms on the table and announced we should get a good night's sleep.

"But it's still early," Minky complained with a whiny child-like voice. Her fingers reached out to touch James' wrist.

He pulled his arm away and gave her a tight smile. "It's gone ten and you all need to be up at six-thirty."

"Six-thirty." I almost choked. "Like six-thirty in the morning?"

"Yes, Luisa." James grinned. "In the morning."

"Yes, Luisa," Minky echoed. "I'm up at six thirty every morning. It's the best time of the day, isn't it, James?"

"I don't know about that," he groaned. "I much prefer six thirty in the evening."

"I'm not weird then?" I asked, falling into step next to him as we left the cabin.

"Nope, not one bit."

When I glanced at him, he was smiling. "Good to know."

As we walked outside, James and I were pushed to the back of the line and I almost yelped when he grabbed my hand.

"Hey, Luisa," he said, sounding hesitant. "Can I have a quick word."

My heart pounded in my chest wondering what he was going to say. After the comment about his six inches, excitement bubbled inside of me at the prospect of our conversation.

"I just wanted to apologise about earlier."

I frowned. "Earlier?"

"Yeah," he replied and scratched the back of his neck. "I think I was a little inappropriate."

So, we *were* going to talk about the six inches, but not in the context that I'd hoped.

"It's fine," I said, waving him away. "We were just larking around."

"Maybe." He sighed and looked at me through his thick lashes. "I shouldn't have said what I did, though."

I forced out a smile. "I wasn't upset or offended in any way." Quite the opposite. It had given me a little frisson of excitement. The most I'd had in a long time.

"You sure?"

"Absolutely." I nodded, smiling through my disappointment. "No offense whatsoever."

James looked over to the rest of the group who were milling around the two cabins. "We should get going. We've got an early start in the morning."

The disappointment was palpable and yet I had no idea what I was disappointed about. It had been one flirtatious comment that had made me feel good.

"And, Luisa," James said, tapping my forearm with two fingers. "You're going to be fine tomorrow. Just take it at your own pace. Don't try and keep up with everyone else."

The disappointment doubled. Not only did he regret flirting with me, but he also expected me to be crap tomorrow. I probably would be, but the fact that James expected it was frustrating.

"Oh, I know," I replied. "But you never know, I may surprise you."

He raised an eyebrow and his top lip twitched. "Oh, believe me," he said, "I'm sure you will."

As he walked away, I couldn't help but wonder if he hadn't just flirted with me again, which only confused me more.

CHAPTER EIGHT

The early morning was not my favourite time of day. Especially when it was drizzly and cold, and I was dressed in Lycra.

I had totally underestimated how I would feel standing amongst three fit, slim women and five hot men with hard-edged muscles. The words overstuffed sausage came to mind. Minky was dressed head to toe in designer sports gear—white designer sports gear. There were already splashes of mud up her calves. She was going to be filthy by the end of the day and I could only imagine what a boil wash would do to the brightness of her whites.

James was looking mighty fine and braving the weather wearing a vest. Showing off his biceps which tensed as he clapped and then rubbed his hands together.

"Are we ready for this?" He grinned at all of us in turn and when his eyes met mine I was sure I saw a hint of pity.

Wrapping my arms around my middle I rolled my eyes. "It's a bit early and a bit cold."

"You'll soon get warmed up," James replied.

"What are we doing first?" Olly asked, jumping up and down on the spot, looking like he was raring to go.

"A quick warm up. A two-mile jog through the woods."

"Quick! Two miles!" I was already out of breath, and I'd only tied my laces. "I can't run for *two* miles."

"It's a jog, Luisa," he said with a soft smile. "I'm not expecting you to sprint."

"Don't hold us back," Minky groaned. "We want to be able to do more than a gentle run today, you know."

"Everyone goes at the pace they're capable of," James said in a warning voice. "We've got plenty of time and I won't have anyone put under pressure." He looked at each of us in turn. "Is that clear?"

"You'll be waiting for me," Romy said. "I told you I have no stamina."

"Bless you, Romy," I replied. "But I think we all know it'll be me that comes in last."

"Slow and steady wins the race," Will said, nudging me. "Isn't that right, Luisa."

"There better not be anything slow and steady about you," Saffron quipped earning a laugh from everyone.

I looked at Will who was blushing, but with a huge smile as he gazed at Saffron. It appeared that the attraction was entirely mutual.

"Okay, let's have a quick warm up," James said in a no-nonsense attitude. "Shake out your limbs to start off with."

As James led us in our warm up, my stomach churned at the prospect of not just having to run, but also holding everyone back. I hated the idea of it all. I hated the thought that I might not be able to breathe. I could barely climb the three flights of stairs up to the office where I worked without needing oxygen at the top.

We did a series of stretches and some star jumps—which

made me realise my sports bra didn't have nearly enough support in it—and we were ready to go.

"Two miles, at your own pace along the path, which is marked with the yellow markers in case you lose sight of the group."

Minky snorted and looked in my direction, which made me bristle. I was suddenly determined to finish as close to everyone else as I could.

We started off at a gentle pace, but it soon became clear that a certain blonde was determined to go as fast as possible. As her legs stretched out I began to lag behind, Patrick and Saul slowed down and called words of encouragement over their shoulders. It was obvious, though, they were finding it difficult to run so slowly.

"Go," I gasped, waving them away. "I'll be fine. Jus… shit… go."

"Are you sure?" Saul asked, running backwards.

"Yes, go."

James appeared at their side, having run back from the front. "Go on, lads, I'll stay with Luisa."

I wanted the ground to swallow me up with the huge embarrassment of it all. Everyone felt sorry for the curvy girl who could barely run.

"I'm fine," I protested. "I'll catch you all up."

James smiled and jogged to my side. "Come on, we'll do this together."

"Honestly, you don't have to."

"You're doing brilliantly, and only another mile to go."

Jesus. I really was going to die. One bright light, at least James would be there to give me the kiss of life.

"Well done," James said, his hand between my shoulder blades. "You did really well."

Bent over, hands braced on my knees, and gasping for breath, I wasn't so sure. Halfway round I'd considered faking a faint so I wouldn't have to finish.

I looked up at him. "I... don't... know... if... I... will... survive... the... night."

James' palm rubbed a warm path along my spine for a few seconds before patting my back and giving me a consoling smile. Like he also might be worried about my survival.

"Okay, everyone, let's make our way over to the clearing by the cabins."

"I'm not sure she'll make it," Minky scoffed, crossing her arms over her chest and nodding at me.

I didn't even have the energy to scowl at her and her unmoving breasts—they hadn't bounced one inch when she ran.

"I'll be fine," I replied, waving her away while wishing I could just go back to the cabin and sleep.

"What's next?" Patrick asked.

"An obstacle course." For some reason, James seemed to think it was a good thing, by the way he was grinning at us.

"Obstacle course?" I groaned.

"Yes!" Patrick bounced up and down on the balls of his feet. "Bring it on."

"Do you think maybe she should take a rest?" Minky suggested.

"I do have a name." I finally managed the energy to narrow my eyes on her, before turning back to James. "How hard is it?"

"Well, it's not SAS standard."

"I bet it is for me." My shoulders slumped as

despondency swept over me. There was no way I'd be able to complete an obstacle course.

"You'll be doing it in pairs so—"

Before he'd had time to finish, Minky had grabbed Patrick and tugged him against her side, yelling, "We're a team."

Patrick frowned and looked over at Saul who shrugged before throwing an arm around my shoulder.

"Me and you, babe?" he asked.

"Really?"

"Yep, really."

While I contemplated why he would possibly want to partner with me, we were forced apart. James pushed through us and cleared his throat.

"Right, can we get started?"

Saffron quickly moved over to Will, while Romy fluttered her eyelashes at Olly. Who, it had to be said, looked more petrified than Will and he was being pursued by a cougar with a clear intent to bed him.

James turned to me and placed his hands on my shoulders. "Take it at your own pace. You're not as far on in your fitness as everyone else."

I liked that he was looking out for me, but...

"Oh right, so you're already assuming I'm going to be crap at it. Thanks a lot, James."

"That isn't what I'm saying."

Saul's forearm landed on my shoulder. "Don't worry, I'll make sure she's okay."

James gave him a tight smile and scratched the back of his neck. "I'm wondering whether you may be better partnering Will, Saul. You're equal in fitness levels."

"But I'm much fitter than Luisa," Romy protested. She grimaced. "No offence, love."

I shrugged. "None taken whatsoever. You're right."

"I'll be gentle on her," Saul joked.

"What if you have to give me a heave-ho over a wall?" I whispered, feeling more and more trepidation at the thought.

"It'll be fine," he replied, with a wink. "I'll just shove my shoulder under your backside."

"Come on," James snapped, clapping his hands. "We haven't got all day." With that he stalked away leaving us all to follow.

When we got to the clearing and I saw the course and the height of the wall, I feared for Saul's shoulder. If he had to give me a leg over then I was pretty sure he'd end up needing physio. If the course wasn't enough to send me into a panic attack then the rain that had started would. I was not a woman who looked good in the rain. My hair didn't fall into cherubic ringlets around my face, it went frizzy and wild like I'd been plugged into the electric mains.

"Right," James said. "Who's going first?"

When Saul put his hand up, it took everything I had not to run—if only I'd got my breath back.

CHAPTER NINE

It was official, I was the most unfit person on the planet. The most unfit and the most soaked. I was absolutely filthy, covered in mud, my knickers were wet, my bra was soaking and chafing under my boobs, and the river between my arse cheeks was probably not a place you'd find pretty enough to eat your picnic next to.

Saul and I had started first, yet we were still going after everyone else had finished. Minky was tapping her foot impatiently, while muttering something to Romy who kept throwing her dirty glances.

"I'm so sorry, Saul." It appeared having a big fat arse wasn't conducive with completing an obstacle course in less than fifteen minutes. That was how long Saul had been hauling me around, cheering me on and generally doing whatever was necessary to get us over the finish line. To be fair, ten of those fifteen minutes had been disentangling me from the cargo net and then another five to haul me over the wall. When James had joined him for the final push, my mortification was complete.

"It's okay, babe," Saul said, patting me on the back as I ran in and out of tyres. "Almost there." Even he was now totally devoid of enthusiasm.

I swiped the rain from my face and looked up to see the finish line, noticing that James' stopwatch was back around his neck. He'd given up timing us—well, me. Along with everyone else, except for Minky, he was cheering and yelling. All of them giving me as much encouragement as they possibly could. As kind of them as it was, it was also mortifying, and images of school sports day floated around my head. My mum and dad always brought my nan and my uncle Peter with them to cheer me on. All very supportive, except Dad would run along the side of me singing the theme from Rocky—every single bloody time, every single bloody race.

When I stumbled through to the end of the obstacle course, I collapsed on my knees and almost cried with the relief that we were finished. Saul patted the top of my head and when I looked up at him, I groaned.

"Have you even broken a sweat?"

"When your boobs were in danger of spilling out I almost did," he quipped with a wink and a cute smile. "You okay?"

"Yeah, I will be."

James squatted down next to me and took my wrist between his finger and thumb. He lifted my arm and gave me a huge smile.

"Am I dead?"

He shook his head. "No, love, you're not dead. In fact," he said with a raised brow, "Your resting heart rate is pretty good."

"That'll be because I'm actually dead, like I told you." I took my vest-top by the hem and squeezed out some of the rain water.

"I feel like *I* died, waiting for you."

"Minky," James snapped. "That's enough."

Heat rose within me and as my anger spiked I turned my head slowly towards her, like some sort of dystopian beast waking up.

"Do you think you could just give it a rest, Minky." I was tired of listening to her. I didn't need it, especially when I'd almost killed myself just to prove that I wasn't a big fat blob who couldn't keep up with everyone. I was wet, filthy, every muscle ached, and I was not to be messed with. I turned back to James. "I think I'm going to go back to the cabin."

"We're stopping for lunch now, anyway."

I shook my head, swallowing back the emotion. "I just need a break." I glanced over at Minky. "From a few things."

He nodded, blinking away the rain dropping onto his lashes. "I get it. Go back to the cabin and I'll check in on you in a little while."

Without the energy to get to my feet, I accepted Saul's hand and let him take my weight as he dragged me up. Once upright he gave me a very soggy hug.

"You did great out there."

"Thanks, Saul, but I think we both know that I didn't."

"Hey," he said, "One man's greatness is another man's mediocrity." We both laughed and James huffed.

"Maybe we should let Luisa get back to the cabin." He cleared his throat.

Everyone, except Minky, said they'd see me later and I waved them bye. Walking back along the track, I didn't bother avoiding the muddy puddles. I didn't have the energy for that or to wipe away the tears which were silently falling onto my cheeks. Frustration and humiliation, in fact all the horrible feelings which existed, were smothering me.

And I had a hole in the knee of my leggings!

"Hey, Luisa."

Stopping, I swiped at my face, getting rid of the evidence of my despair and degradation. "Hey, James."

When I turned to face him, the smile dropped from his face and he rushed towards me, pulling me into his arms.

"Don't cry. It's okay. You did really well."

"No, James. No, I didn't. I was awful and poor Saul was so good about it."

James' shoulders stiffened beneath my hands. As I'd wrapped my arms around him like I was never going to let go I could feel every ripple.

"And don't let Minky get to you." He tried to pull away from me, but I tightened my grip. Because at the sound of her name, the tears started again.

"She's horrible."

He gave a deep chuckle that vibrated through my chest. "I shouldn't really comment, but then she isn't my client, so…" he shrugged. "Yeah, she's mean and has awful taste in gym wear."

I gasped. "James. That's bad."

He pulled back to look down on me. "I'm not wrong, am I?"

"No, you're not wrong." I laughed through my snivelling and swiped my hand under my nose. "I think they must have some sort of dirt deterrent, too."

James shook his head. "She didn't put the effort in to get dirty. Whereas you." He looked down at me. The hole at my knee, the mud covering me, my pony tail which was more down than up and a huge scrape down my forearm.

"I'm a mess." I threw my hands in the air. "What can I say?" I sighed heavily. "The fact I'm here is all Olive's fault." I rolled my eyes. "She was the one who booked it."

"You didn't have to come, though, Luisa."

"I nearly didn't," I grumbled. "I wish I hadn't bothered."

He frowned. "Why? You're doing great."

"No, I'm not." I scoffed. "I'm terrible and you probably just feel sorry for me." I looked at him, studied him and considered how gorgeous he was. He had a hint of stubble, and his brown eyes and thick lashes were soulful and practically beckoning me to bed. He even looked good with water lashing down on him.

"Feeling sorry for you is the last thing I feel," he said, rain falling from his perfect lips.

I looked down my body, my squidgy belly stuck out, and my hips and bum strained against my size eighteen leggings giving me plenty of padding. I didn't have toned arms, I'd almost died through lack of oxygen, and I was too heavy to haul myself over a five-feet-high wall. All reasons why James would never feel anything but sorry for me.

"Anyway," I said, flashing a smile. "This isn't doing either of us any good, standing out here in the cold and rain."

His hands fell to his sides, and he took a step back. "Sure. Yep, go and get a rest, but believe me when I say you've done brilliantly well today. You should be proud of yourself."

And there were the sport's day memories again.

You should be proud of yourself, Luisa, love. And at least you tried.

I didn't need James' condescension too. It was bad enough being the big girl, but the big girl who tried hard was crappy.

"Hardly proud," I snapped turning away from him. "You should get back to the others."

The ones who can run, who can lift weights, and who can do a burpee without their belly hanging out.

"Yeah, sure." He scratched the back of his neck. "You're right."

I nodded and folded my arms around myself. "I'll see you in a little while."

"Do you want me to get you some lunch?"

"No." I frowned. "I'm not someone who eats my emotions, James."

"I didn't say you were." His eyes narrowed and there was a distinct bite to his tone. "When did I say that?"

He hadn't said that. Ever. Never even insinuated it.

"I'm not hungry." I shook my head. "I just want to get my head together."

His slicked back his soaking wet hair. "Okay. See you later. But don't feel like you have to come back if you don't want to."

Even though I knew he didn't mean anything by it, my hackles rose and I hissed back, "I'll see you later."

When I got back to the cabin I was on the edge of more tears. My throat was itching with the effort it was taking to hold them back. Feeling stupid and inadequate, my chest felt tight with the shame. When I saw my backpack on top of my bed it crossed my mind whether to pack up my stuff and run —obviously I wouldn't be able to run, I'd tried that already and it hadn't gone too well. Maybe I'd grab my stuff and walk quite quickly.

"Shit." I couldn't leave because that would mean I'd given up and I'd promised Olive that I wouldn't. If I gave up, it would prove everything that she'd said—that I gave up on everything. Like she could talk. Anger reared up inside me as I looked around for something to throw. There was nothing in the bloody stupid cabin. My eyes wandered around the room and landed on Minky's bed.

Horrible, stupid, nasty, Minky and her comfy, bloody warm duvet.

I strode over to her bed and with my hands on my hips looked down on it. Then I looked down at myself, at the mud which I was covered in. My eyes then went back to the duvet.

With my heart thumping I pulled the duvet off the bed and threw it face down on the floor. Before I could overthink what I was doing, I jumped in the middle and proceeded to wipe my muddy feet all over it. When there were big brown streaks zig-zagged all over it, I chuckled as I calmly picked it up and placed it back on the bed. Smoothing it down, I grinned, because Minky would never know—unless she pulled it right back of course and then I'd deny, deny, deny.

Exhaling, with tears still falling and a false sense of satisfaction, I moved over to my own bed and grabbed my backpack, pulling it open.

I searched through for a clean, dry set of underwear and another set of workout clothes. It would be so easy to get into my bed and stay there for the afternoon, but the desire to prove people like Minky wrong was strong. It occurred to me that maybe I should have just stayed for lunch but the despair at that moment had been too much.

I was just about to take my wet clothes off when the cabin door swung open. I gasped in shock when I saw James standing there.

"I said I'd be fine," I offered.

He was breathing heavily as he closed the door on the rain still pelting down outside. As his chest rose and fell in a deep rhythm he strode purposefully towards me.

"I know what you said." He shook his head. "But I hated letting you walk away."

"Why?" The question was asked quietly.

His eyes were darker and more penetrating than usual, creating an air of trepidation.

"Because…" Inhaling deeply, he took another step closer. "Because I wanted to do this." Reaching for me, he pulled me against his hard body, still soaking from the rain. His hands cupped my face, his fingers threaded into the loose strands of my ponytail, and his lips touched mine, kissing me more sensuously than I'd ever been kissed before.

CHAPTER TEN

A s James' hand snaked up my top, I immediately stiffened. It was one thing knowing I had a few extra rolls but another him feeling them. I breathed in and tried to get back into the magic of the kiss, but it was proving difficult. Thoughts about my body and trying to kiss someone while I basically suffocated myself took the beauty of it away.

His fingers gave my hip a gentle squeeze as he pulled his mouth from mine. "What's wrong?" he asked.

"N-nothing," I lied. "I just…"

"Do you want this?"

God yes!

"Of course I do, but…" I trailed off from protesting I didn't want to be hurt and I didn't want him to be doing this as some sort of pity party. I'd always been determined to be who I was and be proud of it. I hated when people were self-pitying about themselves when it was something they could easily change. Saying to him 'I know you'll get what you want and then I won't see you for dust', was a self-fulfilling prophecy as far as I was concerned, and I didn't want to be that girl.

"You're amazing, you know," James said.

I wondered if he had been reading my mind. When I looked into his eyes all I could see was sincerity. Maybe for once I should just go with what I wanted, not consider the consequences, just go for *it*.

"I know," I whispered and slammed my mouth against his.

What had started off as gentle and soft was suddenly hot and heady. Hands went everywhere, tugging at clothing and winding through hair. I thrust my hips forward needing some kind of release, loving the way the seam of my leggings rubbed against the neediest spot on my body.

James put his hands on my bum and pulled me closer to him. He was long and hard behind his shorts and my heart skittered at the thought of what we might be about to do.

"God." I gasped as his hand went to my boob. He rubbed his thumb across my nipple sending a shiver of pleasure across my body.

"Is that nice?" he whispered against my ear, and I could feel he was smiling.

"It might be."

With a deep chuckle he pushed a hand down the back of my leggings and cupped my bum cheek like it was delicate and precious.

"This bum is just—"

"Fat."

James pulled back. "Don't do that." He shook his head. "Don't put yourself down." He gave my bum another squeeze. "I was going to say it's fantastic."

"Hardly." I laughed. "Not what you're used to."

"It's what I like though, Luisa." His mouth came back to

mine and as we kissed he moved me backwards. "I think we need to get out of these wet clothes, don't you?" Then he paused and looked down at me. "As long as you want to."

"I think it would be a good idea." As I took his vest top and pulled it up, my fingers grazed his firm, ridged abs and I wondered what it might be like to run my tongue over them.

We took another step back as I pulled James' top over his head, and with a chuckle he did the same to mine. When I ran a finger along the waistband of his shorts, he gave a deep groan, and it reverberated through his chest to mine.

"Luisa," he said on a gasp, "I really need to get you naked."

"Okay."

For a moment I got back inside my head and considered pushing him away and making up some excuse, like my period had arrived. I wouldn't be that girl, though. I wasn't some shy, inexperienced girl. I wanted it. I was going to accept it for what it was; that James wanted to have sex with me.

Nodding at my response, he reached around me, pulling the shower curtain back and switching on the water. "I hope it's hot."

I couldn't answer because he instantly kissed me again. His tongue dualling with mine as his hands moved around my body, touching any part he could reach. When I started to push his shorts down, James' hands went to my leggings and did the same. We both toed off our trainers and kicked our clothes away. Not wanting to wait any longer and forgetting to worry that I was standing in front of a seriously hot man in just my big knickers and a sports bra, I divested myself of the rest of my clothes. When James didn't move but stood and watched me, I paused.

"W-what?"

He shook his head. "I just want to look at you. You're so fucking sexy."

My skin heated up and I could practically feel the colour creeping up my neck and to my cheeks. No man had ever really looked at me like that before. Okay, they'd looked at me, but it felt like James was actually *seeing* me. Noticing that despite there being more of me it was still beautiful.

When I took a deep breath, James wasted no time in stripping himself naked. Not just down to his undies, but absolutely naked.

Bloody hell he was magnificent. His dick was long, smooth and a really nice girth size. Because, let me tell you, girth size was important. Too girthy was not pleasant. Some people thought because you were a bigger girl you naturally had an enormous vagina, when my vagina was actually a normal size. It definitely would not take something the size of a small thermos flask.

He was very hard, too, and my heart swelled with pride because it was down to me.

"I'm sorry about my knickers," I said.

James grinned. "Believe it or not, I like them."

"You liar." I burst out laughing. "They're ugly."

He shook his head. "They're not that bad. Honestly. In fact," he said taking a step closer and looking me directly in the eye, "they're a real turn on, but I do think you should get them off."

I didn't need to second guess his request as I quickly whipped them down and kicked them next to my leggings. Immediately my hands went to my bra top, and I pulled it up and off. I resisted the urge to cover myself with my arms.

"Fucking beautiful," James murmured as he practically pounced on me like a cheetah jumping on its prey.

His powerful arms wrapped around me as he walked me

backwards into the steam of the shower. When he bent his knees, for one awkward moment I thought he might be about to try and pick me up. Dread rolled in my stomach at the idea that he'd fail and realise that I really *was* as heavy as I looked. When instead he dropped to his knees I heaved a sigh of relief, and, as his mouth went to my stomach I gasped. James looked up at me through his lashes and the water pounding down on us and smiled. It wasn't mocking due to the size of my stomach, or sad because it wasn't flat. It was reverent.

"James, I—"

"No, Luisa. You're beautiful." He kissed the curve of my belly. "So fucking beautiful."

I didn't care if he didn't mean anything that he was saying or doing, or if he ghosted me afterwards. I didn't care because at that moment he *was* making me feel beautiful. More beautiful than I'd ever felt before.

When his lips moved to the inside of my thigh, I inhaled sharply and pushed my fingers into his hair. His kisses moved down my leg, across to my other thigh, holding me close with his hands on my bum. He added a little bit of teeth, nipping and adding a soothing kiss to my skin, and it felt blissful. I was getting wetter and wetter, not just from the shower, with every touch of his lips and my moans were getting louder.

Suddenly he grabbed my hand and tugged on it. "I don't suppose you have a condom do you?"

I almost collapsed with the disappointment. "No. Shit."

His shoulders sagged for a moment but then he grinned. "No problem, there's other ways I can make you scream."

"But I wanted to… oh no, wait a minute. I know where there are some." I gently pushed him away and tugged the shower curtain open. I was soaked and dripped water as I reached out and grabbed Saffron's bag. "She has some somewhere." Moving stuff around I looked manically for the box of condoms. "Yes," I hissed and held them aloft like they were some sort of trophy. Throwing the bag back to where I'd found it, I turned to James who was still on his knees with his fingers whispering up and down my leg.

"Yes!" Moving to sit down, he stretched his legs out in front of him and shuffled back against the shower wall. "Here, let me."

I handed him the box and watched as he opened it up and pulled one out, ripping the foil with his teeth. As he rolled it down his dick I stared, fascinated. He was clearly well practiced at it because he was soon shoving his hand outside the shower curtain and dropping the wrapper and the slightly soggy box onto the floor.

"How do we do this?" I asked. "This cubicle isn't exactly huge."

His eyes lit up and he patted his knee. "Come here."

With a gasp my eyes widened. "I-I erm no, I can't."

James reached for my hand and threaded his fingers with mine. "Yes, you can. Please."

With a deep breath I lowered myself onto his lap, my knees either side of his legs and my arms wrapped around his neck.

"Hi," he whispered.

"Hi." I dropped my gaze.

"Hey, look at me." He put a finger under my chin and kissed the end of my nose. "Don't hide from me."

It was easy for him to say. "I'm not."

"Yes you are, and you don't need to." He traced his finger down my breastbone, his hand going towards my stomach and my nerves spiked. Keeping one arm around James' neck, I wrapped the other over my belly, hoping to hide it somehow. Silently, James took my wrist, lifted my arm, and placed it back over his shoulder.

My heart swelled as he kissed up my jaw and whispered, "You feel so good."

He raised his hips and patted my thigh, wordlessly urging me to take him inside of me, so I rose on my knees before slowly lowering myself down.

"Oh shit." I gasped as his dick stretched me in the most delicious of ways.

"Yeah, oh shit," he whispered, eyes closed and a serene smile on his face.

His hips lifted and his fingertips dug into the flesh of my waist as I rocked forward. When my nipples brushed against his smooth, muscular chest the friction of it felt good. When coupled with him hitting exactly the right spot as he thrust upwards, it was so much better than good. The awesomeness of it caused me to inhale sharply and thread my fingers into his hair, grasping it like it was a lifeline.

Slowly and with low moans of pleasure, James fucked me. Taking my nipple into his mouth he sucked it with exactly the same rhythm as his hips. As the water from the shower beat down on us, freedom and abandon were the emotions flowing through me. I knew I would let him do anything or take me anywhere. As we found our pattern, James reached up for my hands and threaded our fingers together, moving my hands behind my back. He captured them there with one of his before moving his other back to cup my face.

He forced me to look at him as he whispered, "You are amazing."

Breathlessly, as my orgasm continued to build, I shook my head, unable to believe him. James grasped my chin and held my head still.

"Yes you are." When he thrust up hard and his fingers dug into me, it almost felt like a reprimand. Yet there was nothing punishing about his action, instead it felt like fireworks were going off inside of me. Every single inch of my skin tingled as wave upon wave of pleasure rippled from my groin and around my body.

"Fuck," he ground out as our pace increased.

"James." His name from my lips sounded like a plea as I chased my orgasm.

Understanding what I needed, his hand moved between us, and he began to rub circles around my wet and throbbing bud. When the tingle and waves turned into a typhoon inside of me, James' hips went faster. He grabbed hold of my ponytail, pulling my head back, pumping harder as his lips went to my neck.

We both came loudly. My fingers gripped his shoulders so tightly I had to have left marks and his lips sucked on my neck so hard he had to have given me a hickey. Did I care? Not one ounce, because in a shitty little shower, in a dusty old cabin in the woods, I'd just had the best sex of my life.

"Wow," James muttered, his lips still attached to my neck.

"Yeah," I breathed out with barely any energy left to speak. "Wow."

That soon changed, though, when the door to the cabin opened and I heard my name being called.

"Shit," I mouthed silently. "It's Saffron."

James frowned and shrugged like it was no big deal. I frowned back and pointed between us miming an explosion. He shrugged again and I rolled my eyes.

Scrambling from his lap, and only affording myself a very brief glimpse of his condom covered cock, I got to my feet and stuck my head around the shower curtain to see Saffron standing just inside the cabin.

"Hey," I cried a little too breathlessly and a lot too high-pitched. "I'm just taking a shower to warm up. You okay?"

Saffron moved further inside, and my heart sped up with panic. "I'm fine. What about you?" she asked.

"Yeah. Yep. Like I said, just getting a warm shower. I'll be back soon."

When she took another step closer, I couldn't help but glance at the box of condoms on the floor where James had thrown them. Flustered and trying to think of an explanation that didn't involve, 'our PT and I just had flipping awesome sex', I was relieved that when I looked back at Saffron her gaze was firmly on me.

"Are you sure you're okay?" she asked, pushing her hands deep into the pockets of her hoody. "Minky was a total fucking bitch."

Well, I couldn't disagree with that one. "I've only got one day left of her." I gave a shaky smile, hoping that she wouldn't come any closer because then she might see James kissing up the back of my leg. "Ooh." He did something with his tongue then which almost made my eyes pop out.

"Sorry, I bet the water is getting cold. I'll leave you to it." She turned to walk away but paused at the door and glanced over her shoulder. "Oh, one more thing."

"Yep." I scrunched my toes and gasped as James did the tongue thing but a bit higher.

"James, make sure you replenish my box of condoms when you finish."

I squealed and kicked my leg out, and with the loud 'oof' that James made I'd clearly landed a hit.

"Fucking hell," he groaned. "My bollocks."

I looked back to Saffron who was grinning widely. "Saffron, I—"

"Hey, you don't need to explain to me." She gave me a

thumbs up. "You go, girl." Then she winked at me. "See you both later. Oh, and I'll keep everyone away for the next half an hour."

"Half an hour?" I looked down at James who was cupping his balls and looked a little pale.

"He's clearly going to want to do you again, love."

"W-what?"

"If the way he's been looking at you is anything to go by then once isn't going to be enough."

"I need a few minutes first," James groaned. "Make it an hour, Saffron."

She then blew me a kiss and left.

"Actually," James said, clearing his throat. "I'm feeling much better already. I reckon we can get a couple more rounds in."

When he did the thing with his tongue again, I made a mental note to thank Olive for making me see something through for once. One litre bottle of Ouzo coming right up.

CHAPTER ELEVEN

D inner was awkward to say the very least.

James had gone back to the training session after precisely one hour and ten minutes. He'd made a very quick recovery from his kick in the balls, and it hadn't affected his performance one bit.

Ten minutes after him, I returned, telling everyone I was feeling much better after a hot shower. It was clear that Saffron hadn't told anyone what she'd found, if she had I was sure Minky would have had something bitchy to say about it. We'd got through the afternoon's exercise fairly easily. I had an idea that James had pared it down especially for me, but not too much that it was obvious that was what he'd done. I'd managed to pull the big tractor tyre because there weren't any weights inside mine and it was smaller than anyone else's. I'd also kept up on another shorter jog through the woods, but I had a feeling that Saffron had told them to slow down.

Anyway, back to dinner and it was bloody awkward.

James and I were desperately trying not to look at each other. Will and Saffron were too busy chatting, Romy was barely saying a word because Olly appeared to be more interested in chatting to Saul and Patrick than her, and Minky was being a total bitch to everyone. It was so bad I was considering joining the party of IT salesmen who were staying in the other set of cabins. Considering one of them was wearing a t-shirt that looked like a naked hairy chest with abs, I was evidently desperate for conversation.

"This food is worse than what I feed my dog," Minky complained as she pushed the chilli around her plate.

"I'm actually enjoying it," I replied.

When she arched a brow and huffed, I knew immediately what she was trying to say without actually saying, 'of course you enjoyed it, you're fat, you enjoy *all* food.'.

"I am too," James said from two seats down.

Shocked that he'd acknowledged me, I leaned forward and turned to look at him. He had a forkful of food paused at his mouth, but when he turned his head to look at me and grinned, my insides immediately turned all gooey. He was all showered, again, his hair was neatly styled, and he was wearing a white t-shirt with worn jeans which hugged his bum very nicely—I knew because I'd watched it when we walked over to the dining cabin.

"I'd have thought that you'd be full," Saffron quipped, taking time out from whispering to Will. "Didn't you eat a full buffet at lunchtime?"

I almost choked on fresh air and wished that I had legs long enough to be able to kick her. If only Minky wasn't sitting in between us. Although at least then I'd have an excuse to bruise her shin. Okay so I wouldn't be going to heaven, but Manky Minky was horrible.

"I did," James said, turning back to his food. "Which only made me hungry for more. A lot more."

Saffron snorted and I gasped. He was being very naughty, but I liked it.

"What sort of buffet did you have?" Will asked, taking the opportunity of Saffron's attention being elsewhere. "When did you go there? Was it when you went missing earlier? How come none of us got invited? Was it those slimy salesmen?" His gaze shot to the IT salesmen's table.

Now he came to mention it, what was I thinking about going over there to talk to them? Who the hell wore a t-shirt that looked like a naked chest?

"Yes," Saffron chipped in. "What sort of buffet was it, James?"

"Saffron," I hissed.

She actually held her hand up to stop me from talking.

"Go on, James, tell us," she continued with a grin.

James didn't lift his head and I guessed it was because he was embarrassed, which was mortifying.

"It was the delicious kind," James unexpectedly piped up. "Very tasty."

I grabbed my glass of water and took a long drink, trying to cool down and also take a breather from thinking about James devouring my all you could eat buffet.

"Can we meet later?" James asked, whispering closely to my ear.

I glanced around and everyone was standing next to the bar while Seth ordered the drinks. It wasn't a huge place, around the same size as the meal cabin with a rustic wooden bar to one side. Beer and soft drinks were in cans, wine in boxes, and a limited supply of non-branded spirits. It wasn't a particularly wild hotspot, but it was fine for a couple of nights.

"Where?"

James' little finger linked with mine as he tried to act nonchalant. Like he hadn't given me two orgasms earlier in the day in a cramped shower.

"Behind the food cabin, around midnight. Everyone should be asleep by then." He looked down at my feet. "And why the hell didn't you have those shoes on earlier?"

"You like them?" I grinned.

"Yep. *And*," he said leaning in closer, "if I should get to visit the buffet again it'd be nice if you decided to wear them."

"James!"

"What? I have a thing for high shoes and beautiful women."

I shook my head, but was internally grateful for the fact that, despite my size, I had slim feet which luckily fit into Mr Choo's shoes.

"Well, I'm not wearing them to meet you behind the dining cabin. Especially when it'll be dark."

"I have to ask why the hell you brought them with you in the first place?" There was a little smirk on his lips as he looked down at them again.

"I bought them a couple of months ago and I hardly ever get a chance to wear them. They're Jimmy Choo." I sighed as I also gazed down at the pink stilettos. "I couldn't resist bringing them."

He raised a brow. "I'm glad you did. They're very… sexy."

I often wondered how the thin seven-inch spikes managed to hold me up without breaking. Imagining wearing them while I had sex with James made them even more my favourites.

"So," he prompted, nudging my shoulder with his. "Will you meet me later?"

I saw Romy and Saffron walking back towards us with drinks and didn't have much time to make my mind up. To be honest, though, I didn't need much time to consider it.

"Yes, okay. Midnight behind the bike sheds."

James laughed and shook his head. "Midnight behind the bike sheds it is."

A little shiver of excitement ran over me, and I began counting the minutes.

———

I pulled my hoody closer around me, wishing that James had his own cabin. It was far too bloody cold and damp to be hanging around the dustbins which smelled of waste food. I was also standing under a light which made me feel distinctly like I was waiting for a punter.

"Psst."

I turned to see that James was walking towards me, now with a sweatshirt hiding his spectacular muscles, which was disappointing. You'd think he would be fine in the cold late-night wind. It was very selfish of him.

"I've had some bad ideas in my time," he said as he approached me. "But asking you to meet me out here is probably the worst I've ever had. It's bloody freezing."

"I know." I grimaced.

He reached for me and pulled me closer to him, joining both our hands together. "I don't really think we should get our clothes off, do you?"

I shook my head. "No. It might affect your extremities."

James laughed. "Imagine if my knob dropped off."

I gasped in mock horror. "There'd be no more all you can eat buffets!"

"We can't have that, can we?" He pushed me against the

wall of the dining cabin and began to kiss me. His warm hand pushed up my hoody and smoothed around to my back, dipping into the back of my jeans.

"Can we move from here?" I asked when we stopped for a breath. "It stinks."

"I know. I really didn't think this through, did I? Come on, let's go and sit in my car." James started to lead me away, but when we reached the huge industrial bins we heard a scratching noise. I squealed and jumped.

"Shit, is that rats?" I gripped his arm so tight I probably cut his blood supply off. "I hate rats. Please don't let it be rats."

"They won't hurt you." Despite his words I didn't fail to notice that he started to walk a lot quicker. "They're probably more scared of you."

"I doubt that," I muttered, reaching for his hand.

James chuckled and rubbed his thumb over my skin which was comforting. Not that his thumb could save me from a big, fat, ugly, stinky rat.

"Ah fuck!" James pulled me back.

"What?" I could hear a snarl and when I looked down I could see the biggest rat I'd ever seen. "Oh my god, it's going to eat us."

"Shit it must have a burrow close by." James pushed me behind him. "She's warning us off."

"Warning us off? She could just kill us by ripping our throats out. What do they feed the vermin around here?"

James turned to me and frowned. "You're definitely a townie, aren't you?"

"Born and bred. Why?"

He started to laugh before kissing my forehead. I mean, it was sweet and everything but I'd rather he'd thrown me over his shoulder and ran.

"Why are you laughing? Why are you not getting us away from that thing." The *thing* snarled at us again, baring long fang-like teeth. "Has it been infected with radioactive waste or something? Look at its bloody teeth."

"It's a badger, Luisa."

I leaned around him and peered at the animal. And, it was indeed, a badger.

"I've only ever seen them on nature shows, but I agree, on closer inspection it is a badger."

James moved and the badger took a pace forward, snarling at us.

"It wants to feed us to its baby," I cried. "It's cornering us so we can't leave."

James snorted a laugh. "They don't eat humans. I think it's just worried we're going to attack its babies."

"Hey, Mrs Badger," I called, poking my head around James' broad back. "We don't want to hurt your babies. We just want to have a snog and a quick fumble. Is that okay?"

"You idiot." He laughed, and it was deep and rumbly from the pit of his chest. "It can't understand you."

I looked at him and frowned. "It might be able to." He turned and pulled me closer, kissing me softly. My stomach flipped at the tenderness of it, and I wondered whether this was actually real. Maybe I was dreaming and the whole bloody obstacle course had been part of the nightmare. Maybe I'd hit my head when I'd fallen off the log beam.

Swallowing I looked up at him through my lashes. I didn't want to look him right in the eye in case I woke up.

"Luisa," James whispered, and he licked his lips. "I—"

Mrs Badger then snarled at us again and we both jumped.

"Shit. We need to go."

"I think we do," I whimpered.

"Okay, let's keep our backs to the wall and move slowly past it."

"What like we're secret service agents and we're tracking someone?" I held my hand up like I was holding a gun and narrowed my eyes. "Do we get code names?"

James shook his head. "No, not like secret service agents. Like two people who fancy a snog and a quick fumble trying to avoid a badger."

"A ferocious badger," I pointed out.

James rubbed a hand across his mouth, but I was pretty sure he was smiling. "Okay, a ferocious badger."

When the animal moved towards us, I ducked back behind James and watched from over his shoulder.

"Don't you think we should just run for it?" I asked.

Another hiss answered that question.

"Run," James cried, grabbing my hand as we ran. "Faster. Come on, Luisa, run."

"I can't. My shoes." I stumbled almost going flying.

"I thought you weren't going to wear the shoes."

"But you liked them so much I—"

"Leave the shoes here."

I gasped. "No way." I pulled James to a stop and bent down to take them off.

"No time."

The next thing I knew I was being hauled over his shoulder and he began to run.

Two things occurred to me.

Firstly, James could not only pick me up, but he could also run with me. Secondly, the badger had gone very quiet and wasn't following us but waddling away in the opposite direction—a fact that I decided not to divulge in case he put me down.

"Oh Gym Jim," I said on a gasp as he picked up speed. "You're so manly."

James laughed. "Oh yes I am, Loopy Lu, and I'm going to show you just how much."

When he slapped my bum I just knew I was going to enjoy every single minute of it.

CHAPTER TWELVE

"Best friend?" I asked, turning in the passenger seat to be able to look at James properly. We were playing twenty questions and were five in.

"His name is Tom, and he is a mechanic. We've been friends since we were eleven when I was sent down a class in French because I struggled with the oral."

My eyes went wide, and I almost choked on air. "I'm not so sure about that."

He wiggled his eyebrows. "I've worked hard to improve." He cleared his throat. "Okay, my turn. First boyfriend?"

A lump formed in my throat as my fingers entwined. "Well, that would be Ben Rogers. Next question."

James frowned. "Was he a twat to you?"

Was he a twat to me? *Was he a twat to me?*

"He humiliated me in front of the whole school." My heart started to thud erratically as the memories flooded back. "So, yes, he was a twat to me."

"Shit, I'm sorry. I didn't mean to upset you." He ran a finger down my cheek.

"Oh, you didn't, Ben Rogers did."

"What did he do?" James took my hand in both of his. "Unless you don't want to tell me."

I shrugged. "I don't mind, it's just embarrassing." The memory made me want to puke if I was honest. At least it used to, as the years had gone on the humiliation had lessened a little. "It was our last year at school and we'd been going out together for about a month when we first slept together. I mean I thought it was okay. Not great but okay. It didn't even hurt." James smirked and I grinned. "It was an average penis, you idiot."

"Sorry, but you know how we men are about comparing size."

Rolling my eyes, I continued. "Anyway, I thought it was okay, but he told his friends that I'd just laid there like a corpse. I didn't. I even tried getting on top for a little while. I should point out I was much slimmer then." James shook his head and frowned. "The point is, I didn't just lie there. He came and I didn't, not until he used his fingers afterwards anyway."

"Why the fuck did he tell them that? What a wanker."

"I know. A total wanker. I think they were goading him about it, and he thought he was being a big man."

"Which he clearly wasn't if it didn't hurt the first time," James said with a wink and we both burst out laughing. "What happened then? Did you dump him?"

I shook my head. "I didn't at first because I didn't know. Not until this meme started to go around school." I felt the colour drain from my face, remembering it as if it was yesterday. "It was a plank of wood with my face on it and this robotic voice was saying 'Give it to me, Ben, Give it to me, Ben'. The worst part was his stupid mates managed to send it to almost every kid in school before showing it on the big screen during end of year assembly."

"Please tell me that then you dumped him."

"I got my revenge and then I dumped him." I grinned and was sure I looked a little bit evil.

James gripped my hand tighter, and his eyes went bright with amusement. "What did you do?"

"I flew a couple of pairs of his white skiddy undies up the school flag pole—they were disgusting, seriously shitty." James grimaced. "Then I made posters of him sucking his thumb and cuddling his teddy when he was sleeping. I mean, come on, he was sixteen. Why the hell would you do that when you know your girlfriend is coming over, even if she thinks you're really cute? Until, of course, you tell everyone she was like shagging a plank of wood."

"What a dick. Good revenge though, although I think I'd have suggested dick pics of his tiny knob."

"Hmm," I shrugged. "I thought about it, but I really hate to break it to you, I wasn't lying when I said he wasn't small. If I'd done that he'd have been able to prove I was lying. Whereas the undies, well, there was no doubt they were his."

"Ugh you didn't do a DNA test on them, did you?"

"No." I scoffed. "His mum had sewn a name tag in the back."

We both burst out laughing and the misery that I usually had thinking about Ben and what he did, ebbed away a little. It was still the reason why I put weight on that summer. Who wouldn't when they ate their body weight in heartbreak ice cream? It was also why, whenever I went out with my friends at the weekend, I drank sugary alcopops so I could get pissed enough to forget my humiliation and prove I wasn't a crap shag.

"You know he was wrong, don't you?" James said once our amusement finally waned.

I nodded. "I do. I don't think I'm a crap shag anymore."

James leaned over the console and kissed me gently, his hand threading through my hair. "I swear, you are by no means a crap shag." When his lips met mine my stomach swooped and instantly I wanted more. I *needed* more. Reaching for his hoody, I pulled him closer by a handful of jersey fabric.

"Think we should practice?" I asked, seconds later wincing. "Although there probably isn't enough room in here."

James nipped at my neck, pulling my hair to give him better access. "I think," he said in between kisses on my sensitive skin, "there's plenty of room," another kiss, "for me," and another one, "and you to practice together."

"Good to know," I moaned, with my head dropped back to give James as much access as he needed.

"Excellent," he groaned. "Now lie back and let me show you what a decent sized dick really looks like."

CHAPTER THIRTEEN

As we walked over to the clearing after breakfast, Saffron nudged me with her shoulder.

"Where did you go at midnight last night?"

I shrugged. "I have no idea what you're talking about." I narrowed my eyes on her profile. "And if I did go somewhere, how would you know because I was sure everyone was fast asleep by midnight."

She stopped walking and swung her head to me. "I knew it was you I saw getting into a car in the car park."

"And what were you doing in the car park?" I asked.

She grinned and whispered, "Did you know that Will has a really nice car for a twenty-one year old." She linked her arm with mine. "I mean, I think it's his dad's but it's still nice. Heated leather seats were an absolute godsend in that cold last night. Really kept my botty nice and toasty warm."

I snorted a laugh, so loud that Minky paused marching ahead of us and looked over her shoulder. Saffron and I also stopped walking and waited for her to say something. When all she did was flick her hair and carry on, we gave another burst of laughter.

"Just so you know," I said as we carried on walking, "James has a heated steering wheel as well as seats."

"Really?" Saffron mused. "Interesting."

"Hmm. It's great for warming your feet on."

"Come on you two," James called from up ahead, startling us. "We need to get started."

"Ugh," I groaned. "I wonder what torture he's going to put us through today."

"No idea." Saffron yawned. "But I'm not sure I'll be able to keep up."

"Busy night, was it?"

She cleared her throat. "Well, I was back in the cabin before you, so…"

I shivered involuntarily thinking about the time James and I had spent in his car. After twenty questions there'd been a lot of kissing—kissing and other things which involved us needing to discard the bottom half of our clothing. It was too bloody cold to lose the hoodies.

We ambled to the clearing and the nerves kicked in. After the obstacle course the day before I didn't want to fail again. I didn't want to look stupid *again*. James and I were getting along. He seemed to like me despite my inability to scramble under a cargo net without taking half of it with me attached to my fat arse, and I didn't want to ruin it with any further displays of ineptitude.

"What's the plan?" Olly asked as he stretched out his arms. "Another course?"

"No," James said. "This morning you're doing a hike."

"A hike." Minky gave a haughty scoff. "And how is that going to get us fit?"

"Fitness isn't just about the body, Minky," James replied. "It's a healthy mind too. Which means you're going to do a seven-mile hike. Each of you will start at different times and will follow a specific route."

"What is this, school?" Minky rolled her eyes. "Or Brownies?"

James chose to ignore her comment and pointed at me, which sent a little quiver through my body. The way he looked at me had the quiver end in my knickers, right between my legs.

"Luisa, you're with Saffron." I gave a little squeak as Saffron slapped me on the backside. "Olly you're with Seth, Patrick with Will and Romy with Minky."

Minky sighed, evidently not happy to be paired up with Romy. I had to wonder why she was so disappointed seeing as she could have been paired up with me. Romy also looked like she'd sucked a lemon but that was probably because Olly wasn't showing much interest in her.

James approached each of us with a map, a piece of paper with directions on it, and a compass. "Here's your route." As he passed them to me his fingers lingered on mine. "You feeling okay today?" I knew what he was talking about but everyone else, bar Saffron, would assume he meant my meltdown after the obstacle course.

"Yes, thank you. Every single part of my body feels like it's had a work out, but in a good way. A *really* good way." James drew in a shaky breath, clearly affected by my words. To be able to get that reaction from him with words made me feel sexy and confident and I loved it.

Quickly turning from us, James moved on to the next couple, handing everything out until we were all engrossed in our maps and route. Once we'd read the instructions, we were to set off at five-minute intervals. Saffron and I were the last to go and I wondered why.

"Are you sending us last so that I won't look such a dick when we actually come in *last*?" I asked James.

"No." He frowned. "I have every faith in both of you," he said softly.

"Bloody hell, James," Saffron groaned. "If I didn't already know about you two that would give it away."

James looked at me and I shrugged. "Apparently we were spotted on the car park last night."

Saffron smirked. "Don't worry, your windows were too steamed up for me to see anything."

James grinned and looked so relaxed about the whole thing that I wondered if maybe I dared to hope. However, I knew better and reverted to self-deprecation as was usual.

"I still think you're worried about me embarrassing you and your PT skills," I said, forcing a laugh.

"That's not true and you know it." He moved closer and kissed my cheek. "You're going last because I wanted to spend a little more time with you."

Saffron ahh'd and I rolled my eyes, nudging her hard with my elbow.

"I'll just be over here," she said, pointing away from us. "Just until it's our turn to go."

"Which is two minutes," James replied taking a hold of my hand. "Are you sure you're okay? I mean, we did have a late night."

"I'm fine. Like I said, I feel like I was worked out in a very good way."

"Okay." He then whispered in my ear, "Maybe we'll give it another work out tonight."

"Excuse me," Saffron called. "I can hear you. I know I'm party to this little thing you've got going on, but it doesn't mean I want to listen to you practically having sex."

"We are not," I exclaimed. "Anyway, you've got your own secret little triste going on."

James looked at me quizzically. "Will. He has a nice car for a twenty-one year old apparently." He nodded in understanding, a smirk on his face.

"Why are we keeping it all secret by the way?" Saffron asked. "We're all adults."

I looked at James, who shrugged, and back to Saffron. "I don't know. I just assumed James wouldn't want people to know."

"Why?" he asked, putting his hands to his hips and looking all Action Manly.

I stopped myself from waving my hand down my body. I needed to start being kinder to myself and stop second guessing people's opinions of me.

"I don't know. I just thought you might because of your job." It sounded plausible enough to me. The way James' eyes were narrowed on me told me he didn't believe it, though.

"I'm not a doctor, Luisa. It's not illegal or morally corrupt for us to be in a relationship. We're not breaking any laws."

I almost did a girly clap when he mentioned the word *relationship*. I didn't, of course, because that would just be pathetic. Instead, I turned my attention to Saffron.

"Why are you hiding what's going on with Will?"

She threw her arms in the air. "Because he's twenty-one and I'm twenty-eight and I don't want that vile Minky making any comments."

Wow, even Saffron who was beautiful, fit, and slim had her insecurities. It just proved that none of us were ever totally self-assured. We put ourselves under all sorts of pressure, no matter what we looked like, what we achieved, or how talented we were. We were never good enough for ourselves, no matter what. Each of us at the camp were trying to make an improvement on the person we already were. Romy needed to get more stamina, Will wanted to get stronger so he could join the army, Seth and Patrick fitter so that they could run the marathon. We all wanted to be better, different.

"I'm sure he'd be very proud to be seen with you," I replied, and Saffron laughed.

"I'm under no illusion that I'll be boasting fodder for his mates. And you know what," she said with a shrug. "So what? Life is too bloody short. But I still don't want Minky to know."

"Okay, ladies," James said, clapping his hands together. "It's time."

"See you in a few hours then."

"We'll breeze it." Saffron sounded much more confident than I felt. "Seven miles is nothing."

Hmm maybe it wasn't to her, but my feet were already protesting at the thought. Nevertheless, I was going to do my best and try and make up for my horror show on the obstacle course.

"Come on, Saffron," I said, slapping her back. "Let's show them what we're made of."

"I have no idea where we are." I looked at the map and realised that I may as well have been reading some ancient hieroglyphics. I had no bloody clue.

Saffron had decided she needed a wee an hour in and had insisted we cut through some woods where she could pee without fear of being seen. She said, while reading the map, which I had since discovered was upside down, that it would cut a mile off our hike, and it wasn't really cheating as we were using our initiative.

Not only had it been cheating but she'd stung her arse on some nettles and we'd gone in totally the wrong direction. How far off track we were I had no clue. All I knew, we'd been walking for over two hours before she'd finally admit that the tiny patch of green on the map shouldn't have taken that long to get through.

"What if we double back?" Saffron asked, taking a step away from me.

I assumed that she might have thought I was going to punch her. Seeing as I'd suggested over an hour ago to retrace our route.

"I don't know. I think we're closer to a road if we keep on going. Then, if we follow that one there," I pointed at the map, "I think it'll take us back to the camp."

"I thought you couldn't read it."

"I can't. It's an educated guess."

"We can't guess, Luisa. We have to know."

I held the map out to her. "You want to have a go?"

"Fuck no. I was the one who got us into this trouble." She grimaced. "And I need another wee."

Sighing heavily, I took her rain jacket and backpack so she could go and relieve her bladder *again*. While she piddled, I checked my phone to find we still had no signal and we'd been gone for almost four hours. Even walking at a really slow pace we should have been back. I reckoned we probably had another two hours of walking, but what the hell did I know? I could have been suggesting totally the wrong route and getting us even further lost.

"Woah, that was a long one," Saffron said, appearing out of the bushes. "Like a bloody elephant."

"Hopefully you won't need one when we get to the road."

"We're going that way, then?"

"I think we should. Besides, we might get a phone signal on the road. Then we can call James and ask him to come and get us."

With a resigned look, Saffron nodded and took her backpack from me. "Okay, boss, let's go."

It was official. Maps were stupid and very misleading.

Another two hours later and we were still walking, and we *still* didn't have a signal on our phones. The road hadn't looked half as long on the map but then I should have realised when the tiny green splodge on the map turned out to be hundreds of acres of woods.

"I think I might need to pee again," Saffron groaned behind me.

"You see," I said with a heavy sigh. "That's what happens when you break the seal, Saffron. You can't stop."

She grunted something that I didn't understand, and we continued walking. Not one car had passed us in the last half hour, and it was looking decidedly black up above. I really didn't want to get caught in the rain again, as lovely as my shower had been.

Looking at my phone to check for a signal, I literally jumped when Saffron yelled behind me.

"Luisa, you did it. You were right. Look."

I looked up, and there, in the distance, on the bend, was the big green and yellow sign for the camp. It was the best thing I'd ever seen—apart from James' penis maybe.

"Oh my God," I cried. "I did it. I read the bloody map." Saffron grabbed my hand and started to jog. "What are you doing?"

"I told you; I need to pee and the idea of baring my arse again is not a good one."

And so, that was why, by the time we reached the cabins, I needed oxygen. At least I was convinced I did. I also needed plasters because I had serious nipple rub, and a towel because why the hell do they make raincoats in a fabric that keeps you dry on the outside but makes you sweat buckets on the inside?

"I… can't… breathe," I just about managed to say as Saffron ran off to the toilet block. "I need help here." Clearly her need to wee was far greater than one to give me the kiss of life, should I need it.

Bending over, with my hands on my knees, I didn't see the rest of our group approaching. Not until a pair of trainers I recognised appeared in my eyeline. Slowly lifting up, grimacing like I'd just eaten a bad Scotch Egg, I was met with a very angry looking James.

"Hey," I waved, still panting and choosing to ignore the way his nostrils were flaring.

"Where the hell have you been?" he demanded. "I was just about to send for the police."

"H-h-hiking." I looked around the group and saw Romy was holding a bottle of water, so grabbed it from her. I uncapped it and drank half of it back in one go. "We got a bit lost," I finally added.

"A bit?!" he exclaimed. "You should have been back hours ago. It should have taken you three hours at most; you've been gone for six."

"I told you it'd be too much for her," Minky whispered at normal volume to Olly.

"I was fine, thank you very much." I mean, I wasn't at that moment because I'd been running, but I had been.

She looked me up and down and snorted.

"I was! I've been running!"

"You should have told me this morning if you couldn't manage it," James added. He looked very pissed off with his arms crossed and his chin lifted. "I asked you and you said you were fine."

I straightened up. Sod not being able to breath, I wasn't being blamed for something that wasn't true. "I was perfectly fine. We got lost that was all. And if you must know, I was the one who got us back here."

"How did you get lost?" Seth asked. "The route was pretty easy."

I turned my glare on him. The little traitor. I thought he was my friend after he'd had my sweaty arse crack around his head to help get me over a wall.

"Saffron needed a wee, so we left the route. We got lost and I read the map and got us back here." James grabbed hold of my wrist. "What are you doing?"

"Checking your pulse."

"I'm bloody fine." I snatched my arm away from him. "I have sore nipples and sweat in places that I didn't know existed due to this bloody rain jacket, but otherwise I'm perfectly okay." I turned around to leave before I stamped on someone's foot.

"Oh, dear," Minky said. "She's off to have a hissy fit again. That's it, go and sulk in the cabin."

I swung back around. "I am not going to sulk." I really was. "I'm going to change my top and put some cream on my nipples." God, I didn't think I'd ever said the word nipples so often in one rant before.

"Well, maybe you should sit the rest of the day out," James said, a little too snippy for my liking.

That was it. I'd had enough. "No. I will not. I am okay. I kept up with Saffron except for when she made me run at the end. I will not sit it out. I will not have my pulse checked. And," I said pointing a finger at Minky, "I am not going to sulk. So, all of you just leave me alone."

It was then that a grinning Saffron appeared and threw her arm around my shoulder.

"Did Luisa tell you how she got us lost and that I had to carry her all the way back?"

Some people were just not funny!

CHAPTER FOURTEEN

L ooking around I wondered how stupid I'd been to offer to drive to the pub. The diet Pepsi really wasn't doing it for me, especially as I was barely speaking to any of my fellow fitness fanatics. Okay, Minky and James were the main ones on my shit list and Saffron, although I was only a little bit annoyed with her. Actually, I wasn't even a little bit, because on any other day I'd have found what she said funny.

"Ah come on, Luisa," she said, throwing her arm around me. "I didn't know they'd been giving you shit about us being gone for so long."

I sighed heavily. "Okay. I forgive you."

"Yay." She pulled me closer and kissed the side of my head. "And don't be mad at James for too long, he was just worried about you."

My eyes went to the other side of the table where James was deep in conversation with Romy and Seth. His gaze wandered to mine, and he gave me a small smile. A little boy lost smile is what my Nan would have called it. I gave him one back and saw his shoulders sag. Maybe with relief that

I'd forgiven him or maybe dismay that he hadn't been given a good excuse to end things. I liked to think the former.

"Look at him," Saffron said with a giggle. "He's got a big grin now."

I rolled my eyes and nudged her. "Oh, stop it, you big softie." She might have been wrong, but I still couldn't help smiling as butterflies took flight in my stomach. "Maybe once he's finished his conversation I'll go over to him."

"Make sure you do. Now," she said, pushing out of her chair, "I'm going to see a young man about his magic fingers."

I looked around the table and saw that Will was missing, which gave me a good idea as to where Saffron was going.

"Okay, go on. I'll see you later."

As soon as Saffron left, Minky shuffled across into her seat and my heart sank. "Hi, Minky."

She gave me a tight smile and smoothed down her skirt. Why she'd brought a leather mini skirt to a boot camp with her, I had no clue—I was choosing to forget I'd bought a pair of pink Jimmy Choo's with me. The point was, everyone else was in jeans or leggings with trainers or walking boots.

"I have a little inkling about something," she said, glancing across the table, before looking back at me and licking her lips.

"And what's that?"

"That maybe you have a little crush on our instructor."

My heart sank again, right down to my toes this time. "I'm not sure I follow."

"Yes you do." She smiled but it wasn't very warm. More forced, like she'd been told she had to if she wanted to survive the night. "You're making it quite obvious and believe me he's not going to be interested if you act desperate."

"Firstly, you've got it all wrong and secondly, I don't think I need any romantic advice. I can manage on my own."

She raised an eyebrow and looked at me sceptically. "Really?"

"I have had sex and been kissed and had boyfriends before, Minky."

"Really?"

"Yes, and stop saying really. It's annoying."

"Really?" she looked surprised, as if it was impossible that she could ever be annoying. Well, *she* didn't have to spend time with *her*!

"Listen, Minky, you have it all wrong. I don't have a crush on James and if I did, I think I'd have enough experience to know how to handle it."

"I'm surprise that you're experienced."

"Why?" I stared at her and waited for a response, but she didn't give me one, except open and close her mouth like a fish. "I understand, now if you don't mind I need to go to the loo." What I really wanted to say was, looking at you makes me feel like I need a shit, but my mum had always taught me to be polite.

"Where are you going?" Romy asked, breaking off her conversation with James and Seth.

"Minky farted and it stinks."

Everyone's gaze swivelled to me. Minky gasped while everyone else started laughing.

"I did not," she cried.

I wafted a hand under my nose and grimaced. "She really did. It's awful. I think she ate something that's gone off."

"I really didn't. Honestly," she protested. "I really didn't."

Grinning evilly, I left and hoped that Manky had got the hint by the time I got back and moved seats.

When I came out of the ladies, James was waiting outside

for me. He was leaning against the wall looking all sorts of sexy.

"You're really mean you know," he said.

"She's the mean one. She practically said she thought I had to be a virgin because of my size."

"She said that?" He glanced at the door that led back into the pub. "Why does she have to be such a bitch?"

"Maybe because she was born that way. Or maybe her mother is actually Maleficent."

He frowned. "Please tell me you've seen Maleficent. Disney?"

He shrugged. "No idea."

"Oh my God, I have so much to teach you."

James pushed away from the wall and stepped closer to me. "I'm sorry I was angry earlier."

"You should be." I crossed my arms over my chest and tried hard to look annoyed. I'd calmed down, though, and Minky being a bitch had helped to redirect my ire to her. "And you should have listened to me when I said I was fine."

"I know and I've checked your route and you actually did eleven miles instead of seven. Eleven and a half to be exact."

"We did? Wow, we walked a long way."

James grabbed hold of the belt loop on my jeans and pulled me closer. "You did. And your map reading skills are second to none." He was smirking and I knew that he was forgiven. "Can I take you out on a date next week?"

I stepped back in shock. "Sorry?"

"God, I have so much to teach *you*," he quipped. "A date is when I pick you up and take you somewhere to eat, or maybe have a few drinks and we talk and laugh and generally have a good time."

"I know what a date is. I'm just surprised you want to take me on one."

He sighed. "I thought we'd agreed that there was nothing wrong with what we're doing."

I nodded. "We did."

"I like you. You're funny and gorgeous and very sexy when you're angry. So, I'd love to take you on a date."

I pretended to think about it before grinning. "Okay, but please don't make it a jog around the park."

"I won't," he promised. He gave me a quick kiss on the lips. "Okay I need to go to the bathroom, so I'll see you back in there."

"Okay." Feeling excited I practically skipped off back to the others. My joy complete when I saw Minky was nowhere to be seen.

———

After fifteen minutes, James still wasn't back from the toilet, and I had to admit I was feeling anxious.

"Have you seen James?" I asked Patrick when he came back from the bar.

"Not for ages." He winked at me. "I thought he'd gone looking for you."

I looked at Saffron who looked decidedly guilty. "Have you told everyone?" I asked.

"It just slipped out when James went looking for you." She at least had the decency to look guilty.

Patrick put his arm around me. "We're all please for you, love. Well, maybe not Minky." He gave a throaty laugh. "She's really pissed off."

I guessed that was why she'd left, and I didn't care. She was grade A nasty, and it wasn't my fault that James didn't like her in the same way that he liked me i.e., in a sex and giving orgasms kind of way. Thinking of those orgasms made me want to go and find the orgasm giver and get him to go back to the camp while everyone else stayed in pub.

"I'm just nipping out," I told anyone who was listening. I headed for the bathrooms wondering if James had hung around outside to make a call.

When I pushed through the doors into the hallway I stopped dead in my tracks. My heart stopped before flaring into pain and nausea bubbled in my stomach. James was against the wall where he'd waited for me, but Minky was pushed up against his chest, her arms around his neck and they were snogging like it was an Olympic event. I didn't stop to question or argue, I turned and ran back to my car and drove all the way home, not even bothering to pick up my stuff from camp.

CHAPTER FIFTEEN

I t was official, I smelled. It was a mixture of cheese and onion crisps, hand sanitiser, and hummus. The hand sanitiser being an alternative to showering.

It had been two days since I'd run away from camp, and I'd ignored the twenty calls and ten text messages which flashed up from Gym Jim. *Two days* that I'd called in sick at work because I was... heartbroken was too big a word... heart hurt and pride dented were probably more appropriate.

I'd cried angry tears all the way on the drive back from camp. Angry that, yet again, I'd let someone make a fool out of me. Especially with Manky Minky, the woman who had been nothing but horrible to me. Especially after I'd had sex with him in a grotty shower with a minging shower curtain. *Especially* after I'd had sex with him in a grotty shower with a minging shower curtain *when* I'd only known him a couple of weeks.

The worst part about it was, I was beginning to enjoy working out and getting fitter. I really didn't want to start at another gym, but I supposed I would have to. There was no way I could face James ever again, for the rest of my life.

"Tit," I muttered, not sure whether I was talking about myself or James. "Absolute, bloody, buggering, shitting, tit."

Picking up the remote control, I flicked through the channels and had just decided on a program about the world's most dangerous prisons, when the doorbell rang. I'd considered ignoring it but whoever it was decided that I needed to hear it over and over again.

My heart skipped a little beat when I thought it might be James, but then realised he had no idea where I lived—not unless he'd checked my application form and I doubted that. Checking the camera on my phone, I almost burst into tears when I saw it was Olive.

As soon as I yanked the front door open I practically jumped into her arms.

"I'm so glad you're back," I cried, burying my face in her neck.

"Whoa," she soothed. "What's wrong? What's the matter?"

"I've made such a fool of myself, Ol."

"Oh dear." She held me at arm's length and looked me in the eye. "Please tell me you didn't fart and follow through again."

"That was just the once," I protested. "And the bus driver was extremely understanding."

"What is it then?" she asked as she manoeuvred me back towards the living room. "Tell me all about it."

As we moved, something clanked against the wall. "Do you have wine?" I sniffled.

"No love, I have something much better."

I gasped. "You have Ouzo?"

"Yep. I owed you, remember?" Olive grinned and pointed the bottle at the sofa. "Take this, sit, and I'll get the glasses."

Tightening my dressing gown belt, I hugged the bottle of

Ouzo to me like it was a lifeline. When Olive came back with two pint glasses, I knew we were in for a long night.

"How was Miami?"

She stared back dreamily, and it was clear that Miami had been a damn sight better than the Welsh countryside.

"A lot of sex then."

Olive nodded and sighed as she plonked herself down next to me. "He is so good, Lu. So very good." She giggled and I rolled my eyes not feeling interested in romance at that moment. "Something else happened, too."

I gasped and grabbed the hefty glass of Ouzo that she'd poured for me. "You didn't let him do you up the bum did you?"

Olive gagged. "God no."

"What then?"

Like some giggly schoolgirl, she hid her face and stamped her feet up and down, while jumping in her seat.

"Oh, for goodness' sake, just tell me," I begged, after what had to be two minutes of watching her.

"We said I love you to each other." She clapped her hands. "And he said it first."

My black, shrivelled heart actually swelled for her. I knew how much she liked Daniel and how long she'd liked him, so to know she might have got her happy ever after made me happy too.

"Ol, that's amazing." I practically jumped into her arms, hugging her tightly. "I'm so happy for you." Suddenly a thought hit me, and I let her go. "Are you moving to London?"

"We haven't got that far." The way she glanced away from me told me there was more to it, but I didn't have the energy to think about it. "Anyway," Olive said, distracting me from the thought of her leaving me, "tell me what's wrong.

Why do you smell of cheese and onion crisps, hummus, and hand sanitiser?"

God, she was good.

"Well?"

"I had sex with James in a grotty shower with a minging shower curtain and a few days later he kissed someone else."

"Oh shit." Olive reached for the Ouzo and filled up the glass to the rim.

"You do it," I slurred, passing my phone to Olive. "I can't."

"I'm not doing it." Nevertheless, she made a grab for my phone, but being drunker than drunk, missed it. "When did you get two phones?"

I tilted my head to one side and looked. She was right. "I don't know. Where did that come from?"

"Oh shit. There's two of you, too." Olive sat back and stared at me through one eye. "Yep, two Luisa's, too."

"What?" I gasped and slapped a hand over my face. "I can only feel one of me."

"Nope... oops, sorry didn't mean to belch."

"It's okay, but *you* need to *do it*."

"Fine. Okay. Pass me one of the phones."

I threw the one in my hand, not sure where the other one was, but relaxed when I saw Olive had them both. Sitting up on my knees, I ditched my dressing gown feeling hot and bothered as Olive dialled the number.

"Ohmagod, ohmagod, ohmagod, it's ringing."

Water flooded my mouth as the feeling I was about to puke increased, so I took a quick swig of Ouzo and willed the vomit back down.

"Oh hello, is that James?" Olive said, sounding like she'd

been constipated for weeks and had taken elocution lessons. "No, it's not Luisa." She threw her hands in the air and mouthed, 'what do I say?'

I shrugged. "I don't know," I mouthed back before collapsing into fits of giggles.

"I don't know who Luisa is, I'm sorry… no, I don't know how I got her phone…"

I couldn't stop laughing that Olive was continuing to pretend to be someone else, when clearly we'd forgotten the fact that he'd have my number in his phone.

"I need to wee," I gasped, lying back on the sofa crossing my legs, as the laughter continued to build.

"I can't let you speak to her because I don't know who she is."

Oh my God, the accent was getting even more exaggerated. As it did, my snorts of amusement got louder and my need to go to the toilet got stronger.

"No, I haven't stolen her phone… No, you don't need to call the police—"

That was enough for me to explode and I'm ashamed to say I let a little bit of pee come out. Olive looked at me in horror and promptly threw the phone in the air like it was a hand grenade about to go off. It went up in the air, did a loop the loop and landed in my pint of Ouzo. *Then* I actually wet myself.

CHAPTER SIXTEEN

I couldn't believe I was about to do what I was about to do.

"Dildo."

"Lumpy."

The stupid prick grinned at me like I found his name for me amusing. Okay, I called him Dildo first and Lumpy was his comeback, but he was still a prick.

"Good weekend?" he asked, sitting back in his chair making it rock. "Too much booze?"

"No," I snapped. "I went to a boot camp and picked up a virus." It was actually a PT instructor I'd picked up, but virus suited him just as good.

"Just assumed that you'd had three days off with alcohol poisoning."

"No." Okay, so I'd had one day off with alcohol poisoning but the other two had been because of a hurt heart. Which was why I was about to do something I might just regret for the rest of my life.

I sat at my desk, moved my keyboard to the exact position I liked, turned on my PC, and laid my hands flat on my knees.

"Dildo," I said, swivelling my chair to face him, "I need to ask you something."

He mirrored my position and smirked. "Do you really, Lumpy? And what would that be?"

"The thing is, Dild, sorry, Dylan, I could do with a favour."

"And why would I help you, Lump? Sorry." He smirked again. "Sorry, Luisa."

"Because," I said on a sigh, "I will pay you fifty quid to do it."

He frowned. "Well then that's not a favour, is it? That's a transaction."

God he was such a donkey head. "I suppose it is. That doesn't matter though, what does is if you'll help me."

"It depends on what it is and whether I think it's worth more than a fifty or not."

It probably was worth more than a fifty but to *me* not him, *if* he said yes. It wasn't just fifty pounds I needed to persuade me to go ahead, I needed a brain transplant and a whole vat of Ouzo—although I was still in feeling a little off about Ouzo just now.

I took a deep breath. "I can't believe I'm about to ask this," I said to the ceiling and particularly the fly buzzing around in the casing of the overhead strip light.

"Ask away, Mi Amigo."

I was actually sick in my mouth. The man was extraordinarily hot, but he was also extraordinarily disgusting, cheesy and prickish.

"I want you to pretend to be my boyfriend." I shuddered as the words felt poisonous on my tongue. "I will pay you fifty to act like you… shit, this is awful…"

Dildo raised an eyebrow and smirked. "You want me to

pretend to be your boyfriend, and you will pay me fifty quid to do it."

"Yep." I gave a single nod. "That's about it."

After our failed attempt at pranking James on the phone, Olive and I had passed out on the sofa. When we woke up the next morning we came up with the plan to make James jealous. We were dressing it up that it was to look like I'd moved on, but we both knew what it was really was. Good old fashioned 'operation jealousy'.

Why would I go ahead with such an idiotic plan, you might ask? Because bloody Olive made me promise and she knew when I promised her, I never went back on it.

"Fifty quid doesn't sound like much for that kind of trauma," Dildo said, steepling his fingers under his chin. "Especially if I have to touch you in some way." He grimaced like he'd just been Dirty Sanchez'd.

"Believe me, it's not going to be any sort of picnic for me either."

He stretched his arms and flexed his ridiculously nice biceps beneath his white work shirt. "I won't have sex with you."

I almost choked. "What? No! There will definitely be no sex. None. At. All."

"I mean if you want to up it to a couple of hundred, I could be persuaded."

The thought was heinous at best. "I think I'd rather kiss a dog's arsehole to be honest."

He winced. "Very harsh, but the feeling is entirely mutual. Tell me, if there's no sex involved, what exactly do I have to do?"

I wasn't sure which was the worst part of the plan; having to ask Dildo because he was the best looking man I knew or having to go back to the gym to set the plan in motion.

"You like the gym, don't you?"

"I do."

Ugh, he flexed his biceps and bounced his pecs under his shirt. Like I said, donkey head!

"You need to come to the gym with me and pretend you're my boyfriend. You need to flirt with me and generally treat me like a princess while we are there."

"Okay." He paused as he thought about it. "Can I look at your arse? Because to be fair, you have a cracking arse. Slightly bigger than I'm used to in my partners but cracking nevertheless."

I seriously needed to bathe in bleach when this was all over.

"If the plan requires it for best effect, then yes," I replied, doubting my own sanity and self-esteem, "you can look at my bottom. No touching, though."

"Don't worry, that won't happen. Looking is one thing but touching is another. That would be another tenner at the very least."

I sat back in my seat and studied him. "You are aware that men have moved on mentally and emotionally since they hunted dinosaurs and dragged their women around by their hair."

I realised I wasn't helping the cause by asking a man to help me make another *man* jealous. I also realised I was a strong woman who could easily handle seeing James again. I was hurt, though, and even the strongest people did stupid things when they were hurt. Besides which, I'd still been slightly pissed when I agreed it was a great plan.

"It will be a one off," I said. "We go to the gym, and you do what's necessary to make him think I've moved on."

"Ah, so you are trying to make someone jealous."

"No. I want him to think I've moved on. That's all."

He smirked. "I think you're lying, but—"

"No, I'm not. Now, do you want to do this or not?"

"Can't I persuade you to up it to a hundred?"

"No, you can't." I moved back to my desk and wiggled my mouse, bringing my computer back to life. "And you need to improve your call times as well. You're taking too long and bringing the team stats down."

Dildo raised a brow, gave a little chuckle and started work, while I wondered how on earth I was going to cope seeing James again.

CHAPTER SEVENTEEN

When Dildo's car pulled up next to mine I groaned inwardly. What the hell was I doing? Why on earth had I asked a man who had flames painted up the side of his car to pretend to be my boyfriend? All because I'd had some ridiculous ideas about another man I barely knew. A man who had never promised me anything except to get me fit.

I hadn't had any text messages or missed calls from James in the last couple of days, so I guessed we were done. He had completed the obligatory chasing period of three days and his time was done. He and Minky had probably had a really good laugh about me. Me and my fat backside.

"Hey sweetheart." Dildo winked at me, and my stomach lurched. "You ready for this?"

God no. It was the last thing in the world that I was ready for, but I'd already paid him, and I wasn't wasting fifty quid. Besides, I wanted James to think I'd moved on and Dildo at least looked good.

"Now remember," I said, moving ahead of him. "No touching, no inappropriate comments and no flirting with anyone other than me." I swung my towel over my shoulder, making an extra effort to make sure it hit Dildo in the chest. A chest which it had to be said looked very buff in the tight work out vest. His thighs even compared to James', and they were some of the best I'd seen.

When we pushed through the door, whatever flying thing it was that lived in my stomach went crazy. Swallowing back the nausea, my instinct was to run but I knew I had to see it through. Fifty pounds was fifty pounds.

Who was I kidding. I was doing this for pride, no matter how scary it felt.

My eyes scanned the gym and at first I couldn't see James, which gave me a momentary sense of relief. Then I spotted him, he was pushing someone to run faster on the treadmill, occasionally pressing a button on the control panel.

"We're going over to the rowing machines." They were next to the treadmills. "And you need to encourage me and tell me how great I am."

Dildo saluted me and gave me another of his over the top winks. I chose to ignore it and my jack-hammering heartbeat and strode over to the rowing machine, or as I liked to called them, shitting bloody torture machines.

As we passed the treadmill I held my head up high and willed my legs to stop shaking. I made sure that I kept my eyes ahead and didn't even glance in James' direction.

"Shall we use this one, hun?" I said loudly enough for James to hear. Desperately wanting to see his reaction, but also desperately wanting to appear unmoved by being near him, I almost turned and ran.

"Hey gorgeous gal." Dildo put his foot up on the metal framework of the rowing machine and slapped his thigh. "Want to ride this one?"

Resisting the desire to throat punch him, I plastered on a smile and giggled. "Oh, you are so naughty."

Shit, what the hell was wrong with me? I sounded like I should be in one of those bawdy Carry On films that my Nanna and Grandad loved.

I practically skipped over to the rowing machine and plonked myself down on it, throwing my towel at Dildo.

"Happy to hold that for you, gorgeous," he said and flicked it at my arse.

My gaze shot to his and I gave him a warning glare. "Naughty," I bit out with a forced smile.

Dildo grinned and licked his lips, and I didn't like how much he seemed to be enjoying himself.

"You're looking so good, gorgeous. I couldn't resist." He leaned down and put a hand between my shoulder blades. "Maybe after this we can have another workout, but in the bedroom."

Shit, he'd made me vomit in my mouth *again*. It seemed he had a real talent for it.

"Hmm, maybe not," I muttered and started to row.

We spent about five minutes on the machine, me rowing and Dildo giving me encouragement. It probably wasn't long enough or hard enough for a decent workout, but my skin was burning from the fact that James was only feet away.

"Weight machine," I commanded and Dildo grinned, giving me another cheesy salute.

"Hey," he said as followed behind me. "You have a really juicy arse, you know that."

I stopped walking and inhaled a deep, calming breath, counting to ten. "Shut up, Dildo," I said calmly and carried on walking to the weight machine.

"Put one weight on for me," I hissed. "Make it look like you'd do anything for me."

He wiggled his eyebrows. "I think I might at this moment."

If he made me actually vomit on the floor I would haunt him when I died.

"I'll put the weight on," I said, giving him a smile.

"Okay." That proved he was a dick, a real man would have ignored me and insisted he do it. Oh, well, it played into my plan.

I bent down and picked up one of the weights. It wasn't too heavy that I couldn't pick it up, but it was heavy enough that it could hurt someone's toe.

"What the fuck, Lumpy," Dildo yelled. "Why did you let it go?" He jumped around on one foot, swearing, and I had to admit it was bloody hilarious.

"God, Dildo, I'm so sorry." I'd forgotten my vow not to call him Dildo. He deserved it. "It just slipped."

"Well, I think you broke my fucking toe."

As he ranted, I spotted James coming our way in my periphery. "I've changed my mind, let's go to the cross-trainers." I snapped my fingers and pointed in the direction I wanted us to go. Dildo hopped behind me, and I was relieved at having avoided James... for now.

I officially hated the cross-trainer and James knew that, so I was aware that my choice of equipment would probably impress him. I was all about impressing him and making him wish he'd not done the dirty on me with Manky Minky.

"I honestly think it's broken," Dildo groaned.

"Don't be such a baby," I snapped, looking at the ridiculous machine and psyching myself up to mount it. Each time I picked my foot up the pedal moved and by the third go I just threw myself at it. As I landed on it I lurched forward and almost hit my head on the stupid handles.

"I hate this damn thing."

"I think I need to go to A&E."

"No, you don't. Stop being a baby."

He shot me a look that said I was evil, but I couldn't care less and returned with a look that told him so.

"Encourage me and you'll forget your toe," I offered, feeling a tiny bit guilty, but not too much.

Dildo sighed and pressed something on the machine. "There you go, *gorgeous*."

I tried to move my legs. but it felt like my trainers were made of concrete. "What the hell did you do?"

"Just encouraging you, *sweetheart*."

God, what a dick. If only I'd known more hot men. Pointedly ignoring him, I lessened the tension on the machine and started to move. I tried to keep my eyes peeled for James, but the sneaky little beggar appeared from nowhere.

"Luisa." The voice was soft and sent my nerves skittering. "Where've you been? Why did you leave?"

With a deep breath, I stopped the machine and looked at him.

"Oh, hi James." God he looked good. Dressed in all black workout gear with his biceps bulging, I almost jumped him. The memory of him and Minky then slashed across my brain. "Sorry, I didn't see you there."

He moved closer. "I've been calling you. I know you read my texts. Why the hell did you just leave?"

He certainly looked genuinely upset that I'd left, but then he would, wouldn't he? He'd lost a client because of it. Also, I didn't know why I was making such a big deal of it if I was being honest. We'd had sex a couple of times and not even in a bed. That should have told me everything—a bunk up in a shower and the front seat of a car. He hadn't been any sort of a gentleman. Okay, he'd been all man, but no gentleman.

"I just needed to go. No big deal." I hated the words and the nonchalant tone. Of course it was a big deal. He'd made me feel like a fool.

"Go where? And I thought we were going on a date this week. That was the last thing we talked about."

I shrugged, ignoring the way my heart was almost thudding out of my chest. "Just somewhere."

"Is there a reason you're talking to my girlfriend." Dildo moved up to James and put a hand on his shoulder. I didn't miss how tight he gripped it, pushing his fingers and thumb into his flesh, but James didn't even flinch.

"Girlfriend?" He looked from Dildo to me. "*Girlfriend*?"

"Yeah," Dildo said, moving his hand from James' shoulder and stepping closer to me. "It's been what…?" He looked at me, willing me to give him the answer and so I… panicked.

"Six months."

James' mouth open and closed before he swallowed. "S-six months?"

Shit. What had I said? I'd made myself sound like a cheating she-devil.

"So you were together last weekend? When we… fuck." He scrubbed a hand over his face and cursed again. "I really thought I was getting to know you, Lu, I really did."

Then he turned and walked away, and the self-hatred felt like venom poisoning my body.

"Well, that was good," Dildo said with a grin. "And an easy fifty quid. Although," he moved closer, "I'm surprised how good you look in that gear. How about we take this workout back to my place?"

I forced a smile, stepped down from the cross-trainer, and placing my hands on his chest I gave him a knee to the balls.

"Fuck," he groaned. "What the hell was that for?"

"That," I said, leaning in so my mouth was next to his ear. "Was for calling me Lumpy and generally being a tit to me."

"I think you've maimed me for life." He groaned. "First my toe and now my balls are ruined."

"Good. And you should know," I snarled down his ear, "we're over."

"We were never on," he protested.

"Not the point, dickhead. Now, get out of my way."

With tears streaming down my face, I left the gym, determined never to go back and be humiliated by a man ever again.

CHAPTER EIGHTEEN

Watching people get drunk wasn't my idea of fun. Especially when I was miserable anyway. A week before, I was having sex with James, not sitting nursing a diet coke at the leaving party of a colleague who'd been with us for three months. I'd even put a tenner in for their leaving present only to find out that between twenty-two of us we'd raised the huge total of nineteen pounds and fifty-seven pence. That meant the other twenty-one people I worked with were a mean bunch of bastards who had donated on average fifty pence each. Thank goodness for Liberty, our boss, who put a twenty in. It was still crap but better than it could have been.

Then there was Dildo. He'd limped around the office all week ignoring me, just groaning whenever he caught my eye. Funny how he thought his toe was broken yet I'd heard him tell Marvin from accounts that he'd been playing football.

"Are you okay?" Liberty asked, sidling up to me. "You've been quiet all week, love."

"No, I'm fine. It's just been a long week."

"Don't remind me." She rolled her eyes. "The new targets came in."

"Oh dear," I winced. "I'm sure we'll manage them, though."

She glanced in the direction of Dildo. "Some of you will. Anyway," she patted my knee, "tell me who the hell that girl is who thought Dylan was a good romantic option?"

I followed her gaze and could see Dildo kissing the neck of a tall slim girl whose dress just about covered her bum cheeks. She was pulling him to her with a handful of his shirt in her hand.

"No idea, although I didn't realise partners were invited."

"They weren't but you know Dylan." She sighed heavily, slapping on a smile when Kiara, the girl whose leaving party it was, approached.

I used the opportunity of them chatting to start my route to the exit. It was almost ten and I was happy that I'd spent enough time there. Giving a quick goodbye to Kiara and Liberty, I slowly made my way towards my escape. There was only Dildo and his girlfriend to say goodbye to and she might have been a nice girl, but he was a... dildo... so I gave them a swerve. At least I'd planned to, but right in my path was an even bigger nightmare... James. And he was with a couple of his friends.

I had two options, avoid Dildo and bump into James or avoid James and have to walk through the middle of the snog-fest.

"Shit," I muttered under my breath. I looked between the two routes and wondered what the hell I'd done to deserve such shit in my life.

The lesser of two evils was probably Dildo, he was fairly occupied after all. So, with my head down, I strode towards the happy couple. I'd hoped to sneak passed them, but Dildo looked up from having his neck sucked and grinned.

"Lumpy."

I closed my eyes hoping that when I opened them I'd be back in my lounge, with my jarmies on watching Britain's Got Talent or some other crappy TV show.

"Hey, Dil—" I cut myself short, knowing it probably wasn't nice to call him Dildo in front of his girlfriend. "I'm off, so enjoy the rest of your night."

"You can't go yet," he protested. "Stay and have a drink with us."

I gave a tight smile. "No, thanks. Like I said, enjoy the rest of your night."

"Are you going because he's here?" Dildo looked over my shoulder and I knew who he was talking about. I didn't want James to be *who* he was talking about, but I knew it was.

When Dildo lifted his hand and waved I actually felt my soul shrivel up and die. When he called out, 'great to see you again', I wanted to get a shovel and dig my own grave.

I dropped my head into my hands. "Fuck my life."

"Luisa."

I jumped at the hard tone which was right next to my ear. I hadn't expected him to be so close. I hadn't expected him to *actually* come over. At the gym he'd made it perfectly clear what he thought of me. I mean, he was wrong, I wasn't a cheater, but he thought I was, yet he'd come over when Dildo asked him to. Was the man a masochist? Or maybe he didn't care and just wanted to show me he didn't. The most logical explanation was that he wanted to tell me what a bitch I was. I mean, I would if I was him and thought I'd been two-timing my boyfriend, even if that boyfriend was Dildo.

"Hi James."

"Well, this is awkward," Dildo said, laughing when there was nothing funny about it, whatsoever. "You know after the gym thing."

"What gym thing, darl'?" his girlfriend asked.

I waved her away. "Oh nothing."

Her head swivelled so fast it almost fell off. "I didn't ask you."

Taking a step back, I held my hands up. "Okay."

"Dylan, darl', what did you mean?"

"Dylan!" James' brows almost disappeared into his hairline. "You're seeing, Dildo. The guy who calls you Lumpy? Seriously, Luisa?"

"He called you Dildo, darl'. Are you going to take that?" Dylan's girlfriend poked his chest, demanding that he confront James.

"Hey," I said, putting a hand on her forearm. "It's just a joke between me and Dild, erm Dylan. I call him Dildo and he calls me…" I ground out the next word, "Lumpy."

She turned back to me. "Don't touch me, *Lumpy*." Her gaze then went to James. "And what do you mean she's *seeing* him?"

"Oh fuck." I covered my face with my hands and groaned. "This isn't happening."

"Oh yes it is, bitch."

"Hey," James cried. "Do not call her a bitch."

I dropped my hands and dared a glance at him. He was staring at Dildo's girlfriend and there was fire in his eyes. His nostrils were flaring, and his jaw set tight.

"It's fine, James, honestly." I needed to diffuse the situation before it got out of hand.

"She disrespected you." He shrugged. "But then disrespected yourself by seeing someone else's boyfriend."

"Well, if we're talking about disrespecting people—" I started, blinking at James.

"What the hell is he talking about?" The girlfriend shrieked, interrupting me.

"Well," Dildo said. "She wanted—"

"When did I disrespect you?" James cut him off.

"Er, if you don't know, James, then I'm not going to remind you."

"Dylan, what are they talking about? What gym thing?"

"Lumpy wanted to—"

I knew he was about to throw me under the bus. "It's nothing, just a misunderstanding." I turned to James. "Can we talk about this outside?"

He shook his head. "I just don't get it. You told me how awful he is to you and yet he's your boyfriend."

"He's not your boyfriend. He's my boyfriend, you fat bitch."

Woah. That was a step too far. There were certain things that I wouldn't tolerate and her calling me a fat bitch was one of them.

"Now just a minute—"

It was my turn to be cut off by James. "How dare you? That is not acceptable."

"Hey, I love this song." Dildo clearly wasn't feeling the stress the rest of us were. He was now dancing away with his hands in the air.

"Dylan would never fancy you," the girlfriend hissed in my face before turning to James. "Whereas as you clearly have no self-respect, you *chubby chaser*."

And that was a step beyond too far. That one took her down to hell and beyond. I turned to the bar and grabbed the first thing that I saw, and it just happened to be a large jug of Pimm's.

"Oh my… you threw drink over me…"

I looked at her and smirked. "Yes, I did," I replied and as a strawberry dropped on the floor with a plop, I brushed my hands off and stormed out, not even stopping when I heard James call my name.

Life was too short, and I wasn't going to waste a minute more of it on men!

CHAPTER NINETEEN

"Do you think he's a chubby chaser?"

Olive groaned. "How many times do I have to tell you? No, he bloody isn't." She dunked her biscuit into her tea, leaving it just long enough that it didn't drop in. "We've established that he likes you because you're beautiful and you're smart and sexy."

"Did like me," I muttered.

"*Does*."

"Not after last night he doesn't. He thinks I'm a two-timing bitch. Worse still, he thinks I had sex with Dildo."

"He doesn't think that." Olive scoffed and took a bite of her soggy biscuit. "He knows you're not that stupid."

"He doesn't know I'm not that stupid. Because of that stupid bloody plan, he thinks I was seeing Dildo. Why the hell did we think it was a good idea to take that stupid prick to the gym?"

"We?" Olive frowned at me over the top of her mug. "It was all your idea."

"It was not," I objected. "You suggested making him jealous."

"But I didn't say do it with Dildo."

"He's the only fit bloke I know, though. It wouldn't work with anyone else."

"There's Scabby Steve from next door. He's always fancied you."

I blinked slowly, shaking my head. "We call him Scabby Steve for a reason, Olive."

"You could have made him exfoliate first."

"It would have taken a week at least before he even looked fifty percent less scabby. Time was of the essence."

"Very true." She chewed on her lip, clearly thinking about something. Finally, she exhaled. "Okay, it's obvious. We need to get some hotter male friends."

"Maybe you could ask Daniel if he's got any hot pilot friends that we could invite to join our inner circle."

She cleared her throat and frowned. "There are one or two, but to be honest they either live down south or are up their own arses."

I brought my knees up and rested my cheek on them, thinking about the shit-show with James, Dildo, and Dildo's girlfriend. Even if I wanted to talk to James again, put aside the Minky betrayal, I wasn't sure he'd want to speak to me. Not only did he think I'd had a thing with someone else's boyfriend, but he must also think I'm crazy pouring a jug of alcohol over that bloody woman's head.

"I really like him, Ol," I admitted. "I was really hoping that we might become something. I don't have sex with just anyone you know."

She looked at me through one eye. "Kieran Woodward."

I shuddered. "Okay, apart from Kieran Woodward I don't have sex with just anyone."

She held up her index finger. "Liam McKenzie, oh and Joe Henry."

"You don't need to keep mentioning my poor decisions, Olive. It was a difficult summer. I'd been humiliated."

"Shit, I almost forgot," she said too sarcastically for my liking. "It's not like it's affected how you've dealt with relationships since."

I lifted my head, but kept my arms wrapped around my knees. "I'm a mess, aren't I?"

"No, darling, you're just a little ruffled around the edges."

I smiled. I liked that. I liked the idea of being a little ruffled around the edges. It would be my epitaph—here lies Luisa Gordon, she was a little ruffled around the edges.

"You know what you need?" Olive announced. She put her mug down on the floor and turned in her seat, grinning excitedly at me.

"What?" I asked, dread creeping over me. Olive did not have the best record with good ideas—Exhibit A, us joining the gym.

"You need to join a night class."

I shook my head. "No. Not happening." She even got the wagging finger because I was so adamant. "The last thing you signed me up for got me into this crap."

"Yes, but this thing doesn't have any men involved."

"No, Olive. It isn't happening."

"My mum told me about it," she insisted. "It'll be good fun. Please, Lu."

"Really?" I dropped my head back against the chair. "Do I have to?"

"Yes, you do have to. You need a distraction from Gym Jim."

My heart clenched at the mention of his name. I knew he'd been a shit to me by sneaking around with Minky at the pub, but I couldn't help wishing I could talk to him about everything. Find out why he did what he did and if he ever really liked me, or was I just a quick shag?

I didn't even know if he was still seeing Minky. Maybe that had been a quick bunk up too. I'd had a boyfriend once before who'd cheated on me—not that James was my boyfriend—and I'd dumped him the moment I found out and never spoke to him again. Which was why I couldn't understand my desire to talk to James. God, he took up far too much of my headspace.

"What are we signing up for, exactly?"

Olive's eyes lit up and she jumped up and down in her seat. "It's Pole Dancing. And you know what the best thing is?"

"What?" I sighed.

"There'll be not one man in sight."

Well, there was that I supposed.

CHAPTER TWENTY

The rain lashed down as I thought about the pole dancing class, I was about to go to. I was petrified. Not only did I not think I was built for it, but I felt about as sexy as a granny in a thong. In fact, my knickers were probably bigger than my granny's—she was a very forward thinking woman my granny. At least it was a beginner's class and so hopefully we'd all be as hopeless as each other.

Pulling up outside the college, I looked around for Olive's car, but her yellow Beetle was nowhere to be seen. It was only five minutes before we were due to start, and I was concerned she'd done another runner on me. I reached for my phone and brought it to life and, surprise surprise, there was a message from her,

Olive: So sorry, Lu. My mum has made me go for dinner as she was wants the deets on Daniel. Take notes for me and DO NOT SKIP IT. YOU PROMISED xx

. . .

"I bloody knew it." I let out a strangled warble of frustration. How the hell did she think I was going to take notes when I was attempting to swing around a bloody metal pole?

I threw my phone into my bag, grabbed it and got out of the car to stomp across the car park. Once inside there was a list pinned up as to which room the different classes were in. I located where mine was and headed for it. As I walked down the corridor, I spotted another woman peering in through the glass panel on each door. She was humming to herself and giggled each time she looked in the wrong room.

"Are you lost?" I asked.

"Oh hello, love." She placed a hand on her chest and sighed. "I am. I keep getting the wrong room." She giggled. "I don't want to be late, I've been looking forward to this for ages."

"Well," I said, walking up beside her and looking up at the number on the door. "What room number are you looking for? This is eight."

"Ooh, I didn't know they had specific room numbers. Where does it tell you that?"

Her pretty little face fell as she looked up and down the corridor. She was only small, had a peaches and cream complexion and smelled of proper, old-fashioned soap. I guessed she was in her seventies because with her hair set in big curls and her stay-crease trousers with elasticated waist and pretty flowered blouse, she dressed just like my neighbour, Mrs Jenks who was almost eighty.

"Are you looking for flower arranging by any chance?" I asked because it was one of the classes I'd noted on the list. I'd also remembered the room number as backup in case I chickened out of the pole dancing.

I decided if she was going to flower arranging I'd go with her and blag my way in. Sod Olive and her bright ideas, seeing as she'd deserted me, *again*. The lady looked kind, and a much better night class companion.

"Oh no dear," the lady replied. "I'm looking for pole dancing for beginners."

"P-pole dancing?" My eyes felt like they were almost popping out of my head.

"Yes dear. I've been wanting to do it for years." She smiled brightly. "What about you?"

"Me? Oh erm, I'm doing pole dancing, too. Me and my friend signed up."

"Really?" She clapped her hands gleefully. "Your friend already here, is she?"

"No," I answered with a frustrated sigh. "She had something come up last minute."

"Oh, that's a shame. Never mind, you and I can be pole buddies." She giggled. "My name is Carol by the way."

"Pleased to meet you, Carol. I'm Luisa."

"Ooh that's a pretty name."

"Thank you, and so is Carol." I mentally rolled my eyes. I hated the name Carol because I had an evil Auntie Carol who smelled musty and always bought me a subscription to a slimming magazine for Christmas. "Anyway, I think we need to carry on down here, we're in room eleven."

"Good job you know where we're going."

"We could always go to flower arranging if you fancy it?" I offered hopefully.

"Ooh no,' she protested. "I'm really excited about this."

I couldn't agree with her because I had not one inch of excitement in me. In fact, I was more excited about the cervical smear I was booked in for the following week.

"I didn't know what to wear," Carol said as we continued along the corridor.

I looked at her and wondered how the hell she was going

to swing a pole in her polyester trousers. I was pretty sure the friction might set her on fire.

"I'm not sure you'll be able to do it in your trousers and blouse," I suggested.

She giggled and waved me away. "I have a leotard on underneath, silly." She looked at me. "I like your leggings."

They were plain black but had hot pink panels down the side with a matching vest top and were new. I'd had to buy them because the ones I'd taken to camp weren't fit to wear. One pair had holes in the knees from the obstacle course while the other had a big ladder in them from trekking through the woods when Saffron needed to pee. Thinking about Saffron I sighed. I'd fully intended to get everyone's phone number, except Minky's of course, before we left camp. I'd hoped we could all meet up for drinks at some point, but my quick escape had put an end to that idea.

"I think this might be it," Carol said as we reached a pair of double doors.

We both peered in to see a group of about five or six women standing around chatting. I was relieved to see that not all of them were slim and young, Carol being a case in point. With a deep breath I pushed the doors open and we walked inside. As we did there was a lull in the conversation, and everyone looked our way.

"Nope, not them," a tall blonde girl in leggings and a sweatshirt called to everyone.

"Sorry, we're just here for the class."

Everyone waved before carrying on talking, as Carol and I moved to the outskirts of the group.

"I think I might be the oldest person here," Carol whispered to me. "I hope I don't hold the class back."

"You'll probably do better than me," I replied. "I'm hardly built for swinging around a metal pole."

"Well, she's bigger than you."

I winced because although she'd whispered, Carol was pointing at a lady who was at least two sizes bigger than me, but clearly had more confidence. Her bright yellow all in one, long legged leotard had cut-outs at the side and was skin tight and she looked amazing. When she looked over I gave her a bright smile but didn't feel anything close to happy.

"I don't know if I can do this, Carol."

She looked up at me and frowned. "Of course you can. If I can then you can."

"Did you see the instructor on your way in?" the bigger lady asked while hitching some of her yellow leotard out of her bum crack.

Instantly I relaxed, relieved that not everyone was super professional and being on their best behaviour.

"No," Carol replied. "We got lost. Well, I did, and Luisa rescued me."

"We're supposed to start in a couple of minutes," yellow leotard said.

I glanced at the clock on the wall and saw we actually had five minutes before we started. Personally, I would have been glad if the instructor never turned up, but I was clearly the only one because everyone else was looking anxiously at the door.

"I'll give them another couple of minutes and then go and look for them," the tall blonde girl said. "I need to leave on time so don't want to lose any of the hour."

I was more than happy to lose plenty of the hour, and I decided that after that session I wouldn't be going back. In fact, if the instructor didn't turn up in the next two minutes, I was out of there, but Olive would still owe me.

"Carol," I whispered.

"Yes, love."

"I think I'm—"

"Hey ladies, sorry I'm a little late."

My heart felt like it had just dropped through my backside and onto the floor. It couldn't be. Now way on earth was *he* the instructor. Not a bloody chance.

I whirled around and I was wrong. There was a bloody chance. "*James.*"

"*Luisa.*"

Carol giggled and nudged me. "My word," she said. "I can't wait to have him help me improve my pelvic floor."

I didn't wait to find out how James was planning on doing that because I was out of the door without a backward glance.

CHAPTER TWENTY-ONE

"Shit!" I couldn't find my bloody keys and since I'd been inside the college it had started to rain. "Why me?"

"Luisa!"

I lifted my eyes to the sky and cursed whoever it was who'd decided to beat me with such a shitty stick. I didn't need James chasing after me. What was there to say? He'd kissed Minky and possibly more, and he thought *I'd* kissed Dildo, and possibly more.

"James, just go and do your class."

He put his hand on my elbow and his touch sent an electric pulse through every nerve in my body. My nipples recognised him and pebbled beneath my sports bra and vest top. Even my lungs were aware of him as my breath turned shallow.

"No, I want to talk to you."

"People are waiting for you." I finally looked at him and I just wanted to cry. He looked so damn gorgeous dressed all in black with the rain beating down on him. There obviously something about our most charged moments being in the rain.

"I don't care. Besides, there's someone else with them."

"Who?"

"My partner, Caitlin." My face must have said a thousand words because he sighed heavily. "Not that sort of partner. My business partner and nothing more."

"I didn't say anything."

"You didn't have to, your face said it all." He moved to stand in front of me, his hand on the roof of my car. "Can we sit inside? We're getting soaked and there's no shower here."

He grinned but I didn't find it amusing. In fact, I just wanted to punch him in his stupid handsome face.

"Why the hell did you kiss Minky?" I moved a few steps back, wanting to be able to look into his eyes.

"I didn't kiss Minky. She kissed me." He stared at me for a few beats before he scrubbed a hand down his face. "Shit, is that why you left the boot camp? Seriously? I had no idea you'd seen, it happened so quick."

"Oh, I saw you, James. I saw you kissing outside the toilets, of all places."

"Because that was where she pounced on me. If you recall I'd asked you on a date before I went to the bathroom and when I came out she was there. She grabbed me and pushed me against the wall."

I cocked my head to one side and looked him up and down. "Wow, she must be very strong to be able to push you against a wall. I mean look at you, James. You're not exactly a weakling, are you?"

I looked at him and he was gorgeous and manly, and his biceps were nicely bulged, and his lips were kissable, and his hair, even plastered to his head in the rain, was perfect. What he was not was someone who could be pushed against a wall by a woman who stood as high as his armpit.

"She was like a bloody woman possessed," James cried. "I had no chance. I pushed her away as soon as I was able."

"As soon as she'd washed your bloody tonsils you mean."

"No, as soon as I could without hurting her. I told her I wasn't interested and to get away from me. I told her about us and how I felt about you."

My pulse spiked at what that might mean. How *did* he feel about me? Had I imagined it all at the boot camp? Why had he chased after me?

"I swear, Luisa, she kissed me, and I didn't do anything to encourage her."

I sighed heavily. "She knew about us and being the bitch she is, she decided that she'd make a play for you," I informed him. "So, she wouldn't need any encouragement, believe me."

We fell silent and unsure of what to do or say, I searched in my bag for my keys again. The rain seemed to get heavier as it sheeted sideways making it difficult to see and I was getting more and more frustrated, huffing and heaving out heavy breaths.

"Come and sit in my car with me," James suggested.

"No, I just need to go home."

"No, you don't, Luisa," he stressed, placing his hands on my shoulders. "We need to talk about us. About how I feel about you. About why you are letting men like that dick disrespect you."

"I'm not letting him do that."

"You're seeing someone who has a girlfriend. And I can't believe you still care about him after what we had together. What we experienced."

His eyes were soft and pleading as his hand came to face and cupped my cheek. The warmth of his palm against my cold, wet skin was comforting, and I wanted nothing more than to sink into his arms.

"Did you really push her away?"

He nodded. "You can ask the others. She left the pub, and, like, you went home, although she spent the time to go back and pick up her stuff. She even hung around to accuse Saffron of having sex with Will in the woods, on her duvet, because it was covered in mud."

"What did Saffron say?" I asked, feeling guilty.

James grinned. "She admitted that they did have sex on her duvet, but it was on her bed at the time." He shrugged. "So, no idea where the mud came from."

"Maybe she really is as manky as we thought," I replied, with a heavy sigh.

"Maybe." His fingers whispered against my cheek. "Why did you just run? Why didn't you take your stuff?"

Why? Because my heart ached so much I'd totally forgotten about my bags. "I just wanted to get away from the place."

"I have it; your bag," he explained. "It's in my locker at the gym but you threw me a bit of a loop when you turned up with that idiot."

Sighing and trying not to lean further into his touch, I whispered, "I'm not really seeing Dildo. It was all to make you think I'd moved on."

James frowned, dropping his hand. "Really?"

"Yeah, really."

"Was there no one else you could ask to do it?" He shook his head. "Because he's an absolute prick."

"He's the only good looking guy I know." I winced.

Grinning, he replied, "Ooh shallow, Luisa."

"I know, but I wasn't thinking straight. I was upset." I

blinked away the rain on my lashes and took a deep breath. "How *do* you feel about me, James?"

Exhaling, he pulled me closer until we were chest to chest, his forehead against mine and our fingers threaded together.

My heart hammered hard as I waited for him to say something. Anything. But he remained silent for a few of the beats of my heart, beats which I was sure that he could hear. Finally, he drew in a breath.

"How I feel about you is nothing that I've ever felt before. I can't stop thinking about you, can't stop wanting you and wanting to see what we could become. I hated the idea that you were with someone else, especially him. I wanted to kill him for touching you because as far as I was concerned, you were mine."

My heart swelled and my stomach did a full twist, as his words sank in and his eyes shone with sincerity.

"I'm sorry I made you feel like that." Regret washed through me as I considered what a stupid plan it had been. "I shouldn't have done it. It was just… it was just, I thought you'd lied to me, and I don't trust many men, James, but I trusted you."

It was out there. I'd been totally honest with him and myself. That was what had hurt the most. I'd trusted him with my insecurities, my confidence, and my body, and I'd thought he'd betrayed me. I'd thought he'd betrayed *me* with the slim, pretty girl because I hadn't been good enough.

"I know and that's why I would never, ever do that to you. If I'd wanted Minky I would have told you." He wrapped his arms around me and buried his face in my hair. "I'm not that man, Luisa. The one who doesn't see you for how beautiful you are. I do see you, every single amazing part of you."

Wanting to lay claim to him and forget every shitty thing

I'd ever had said about me, I stood on my tiptoes and kissed him. Letting my lips and tongue tell James I needed him, while the lashing rain continued to soak us to the skin.

James' hands went to the small of my back and pushed me closer to him as we lost ourselves in each other, not caring who was watching us or what they thought. As we tugged at clothes, gripped hair and nipped at lips, all the bad that had gone before disappeared. It floated away leaving just us. Me and him.

Breathless, James eventually broke away and smiled at me. "You know you owe Olive a huge debt of gratitude."

"For signing me up to the gym?"

He laughed and shook his head. "No, for signing you up for the pole dancing." I frowned. "She knew I was the instructor."

"How does she know that?" I asked, confused. "She never mentioned it."

"She never mentioned that she knows my brother?"

What the hell was he talking about? "No. She hasn't. Who's your brother?"

He narrowed his eyes. "She really hasn't said. That's how she knew about booking PT sessions with me, my brother told her. And probably about the pole dancing I would have thought. Apparently he showed her a photograph of me, and she thought I'd be perfect for you. We'd be perfect for each other."

"James," I said, my tones insistent. "Who is your brother?"

"Daniel," he replied. "My brother is Daniel, Olive's boyfriend."

It was a good job he was holding me tight because I might just have passed out. "Daniel the pilot is your brother. Daniel who lives in London? That Daniel?"

He grinned and nodded. "Yep, that Daniel."

"Well shit."

"Yep." James laughed wrapping his arms tightly around me and kissing the top of my head.

"Why didn't you tell me?" I asked, looking up at him, my arms around his waist. "About him and Olive."

"I didn't know," he replied. "Not until tonight."

"Tonight?"

"Yeah, when they turned up at my mum and dad's house for tea. That's why I was late for the class."

Bloody Olive. The sneaky little…

"She's stitched us up right from the beginning." I shook my head in disbelief. "She knew I wouldn't go if I thought she was trying to fix me up. If I knew she knew you."

"I know," he said, kissing me softly. "But who cares? She meant well and she was right, we are perfect for each other."

I smiled and felt a whole host of butterflies swarming wildly in my stomach. She had meant well, and I bloody loved her for it.

"Before we go back to your place or mine, can we do something?" I asked.

James frowned. "Sure. What?"

"I need to go and buy something?"

"I have condoms," he said with a grin.

"Oh, it's not condoms." I wiped his soaking wet hair from his face. "I need to get a bottle of Ouzo. I have a big thank you to give."

James shook his head, a huge grin spread across his face. "Anything for you, Lu, absolutely anything."

With my heart full and my excitement levels high at the prospect of everything to come, I knew that I had the best friend in the world and that a bottle of booze would never be enough to thank her.

CHAPTER TWENTY-TWO

James

I had no clue what was wrong with my bloody wife, but she was being a pain in the arse. Today was the day we were signing the contract for our own gym. I say ours, but I doubted that Luisa would go anywhere near the equipment. Her love of the gym hadn't improved over the last three years. She went at times when she was beginning to feel guilty, or for a few weeks after Christmas or before our annual holiday, but generally she stayed away and kept fit by walking for miles with our dog Ouzo—what else were we going to call him? Luisa wouldn't be on the gym floor anyway because she was going to run the admin side of things and I couldn't wait to work with her.

That was if she stopped being moody. She'd been snappy and grumpy for the last few days and if I didn't know how much we fucking loved each other, I'd think she was building up to leave me.

Bracing myself for an earbashing, I moved to the bottom of the stairs. "Lu, babe, are you ready?" I winced and waited but there was nothing. "Lu?"

I heard footsteps and watched as the beautiful woman I loved appeared. She stepped on the top step and halted.

"What's wrong?"

"I think we need to talk," she said quietly, gripping tightly onto the banister.

My heart began to thunder in my chest. My mouth was dry and there was a thick lump in the back of my throat. I actually felt fear because she looked petrified about what she wanted to talk about. Taking the stairs two at a time, I was soon on the step below her. When I moved to take her hand, she turned and walked towards the bedroom, and I followed.

"Lu, you're scaring me. What's wrong?"

"We can't sign the contract on the gym. You have to call Tranter and pull out."

I was going to vomit.

Why hadn't I taken the mood swings seriously? How had I let it get to the point that she was going to leave me?

"You can't leave me," I blurted out. "Whatever I've done wrong, I'll sort it."

She shook her head and my stomach dropped. When she spoke, it swooped back up again.

"God no, I don't want to leave you. I love you, you bloody idiot."

I sagged with relief but then remembered she wanted us to pull out of the gym. "Why the hell can't we sign for the gym? We're supposed to meet the solicitor in half an hour. It's a bit late in the day, babe."

"I know and I'm sorry, but I've been trying to tell you all week."

I thought carefully about my words before asking, "Is that why you've been a bit... erm... low this week?"

She nodded solemnly, linking her fingers together in front of her. "I'm sorry."

Wrapping my arms around her, I hugged her tight and kissed the top of her head. "Tell me why we can't do this."

Luisa didn't answer immediately, and I was just about to prompt her when she took a deep breath. "We can't do it because of the money."

"We've been through it and our accountant has been through it. We can do this and have a decent life."

"We can't, James." She dropped her head and rested it against my chest. "We just can't."

"Why?" I whispered.

"Because," she said on a sigh, "we're going to have another mouth to feed soon. I didn't mean for it to happen. I took my pill, I swear, but it must have been Daniel and Olive's wedding, when I got pissed on Ouzo. I was sick the next day."

The next day and evening if I remembered correctly. But that didn't matter to me. What mattered to me was what she'd told me.

"We're having a baby?" I asked, in awe of the beautiful woman in front of me. "Me and you are going to be parents?"

Luisa nodded with a tiny smile twitching at her lips. "Yes, in seven months. That's why we can't sign for the gym."

"Oh Lu," I sighed, unable to hold back my grin. "That's exactly why we should sign for the gym. It's our future, babe. Mine, yours, and our family's. Our baby's." I kissed her, determined to wipe away her fears. "It's going to be amazing."

"Are you sure?"

"Absolutely. Now, get yourself ready because we have a quick stop to make on the way."

"Where?" she asked.

"Somewhere they sell Ouzo," I replied. "Because we owe

Olive the biggest bottle we can find for helping us get this life."

My wife gave me a perfect smile and I knew then we'd have a perfect life to match.

ABOUT THE AUTHOR

Nikki lives in Cheshire with her husband, two dogs, and lovely mother-in-law who supplies her with endless cups of tea. She writes romance with a touch of humour and lots of love, and hopes that she puts a smile on her reader's faces and a sigh in their heart.

Her ambitions of becoming a writer started at the age of 10 when she started writing poetry at school, and was given the honour of reading one of her poems to the rest of her year group (a truly embarrassing experience that she will never forget).

Nikki is grateful for the wide variety of strange and wonderful people in her life, otherwise, she'd never know what to write about! She always takes a keen interest in family and friends, finding out their innermost secrets in readiness for her next book.

For updates on future releases check out her social media links.

facebook.com/NikkiAshtonBooks

twitter.com/NikkerAsh

instagram.com/nikkiashtonauthor

ALSO BY NIKKI ASHTON

Standalones

(All books are standalone stories, with 'guest' appearances from characters in the previous book)

Guess Who I Pulled Last Night?

No Bra Required

Get Your Kit Off

Cheese Tarts & Fluffy Socks

Roman's Having Sex Again

The Big Ohhh!

Do You Do Extras?

Pelvic Flaws

Snake Bandit (YA)

*

The Curvy Girls Club

(Quick reads for those moments of relaxation)

The OffRom

The Gymfatuation

*

Connor Ranch Stories

(Contemporary Romance)

Box of Hearts (Single Dad, Second Chance)

Angels' Kisses (Second Chance)

Secret Wishes (YA)

*

Cooper Brothers

(Contemporary, Second Chance Romance)

Elijah

Samuel

*

Love in Dayton Valley

(Standalone Romantic Humour)

The Triple Threat (Friends-to-Lovers)

The Jackpot Screwer (Surprise Baby)

The Beef Game (Single Dad, Second Chance)

The Bitch List (Enemies-to-Lovers)

*

Maddison High School

(Contemporary, British High School, Enemies-to-Lovers Romance)

Hate Struck

Love Struck

*

Rock Stars Don't Like

(Standalone Romantic Humour)

Rock Stars Don't Like Big Knickers (Single Mum)

*Rock Stars Don't Like Ugly Bras (*Enemies-to-Lovers)

Rock Stars Do Like Christmas Stockings (Secret Romance)

Rock Stars Don't Like Sparkly Thongs

*

The Warrior Creek Series

(Standalone Rock Star Romance)

The Last Chorus (Friends-to-Lovers)

The Opening Line - Coming 2023

The First Chord - Coming 2024

The Final Beat - Coming 2025

OTHER AUTHORS AT HUDSON INDIE INK

Paranormal Romance/Urban Fantasy

Stephanie Hudson

Xen Randell

C. L. Monaghan

Sorcha Dawn

Harper Phoenix

Crime/Action

Blake Hudson

Jack Walker

Contemporary Romance

Gemma Weir

Nikki Ashton

Nicky Priest

Anna Bloom

Milton Keynes UK
Ingram Content Group UK Ltd.
UKHW010718140823
426838UK00001B/38